MW00458750

Shorts

The Circles I Move In

The Circles I Move In

SHORT STORIES

BY

Diane Lefer

𝒵

ZOLAND BOOKS

Cambridge, Massachusetts

First edition published in 1994 by
Zoland Books, Inc.
384 Huron Avenue
Cambridge, Massachusetts 02138

PUBLISHER'S NOTE

This book is a work of fiction. Names, characters, places and
incidents are either the product of the author's imagination
or are used fictitiously. Any resemblance to actual events or
persons, living or dead, is entirely coincidental.

"Happiness Line" Words and music by Linda Alexander
© 1978 Linda Alexander. Used by permission.
All rights reserved.

"Don't Tell Me the Bad News" Words and music by Pipp
Gillette. © 1980 by Lucy's Store Music. Used by permission.
All rights reserved.

FIRST EDITION

Book design by Boskydell Studio
Printed in the United States of America

01 00 99 98 97 96 95 94   8 7 6 5 4 3 2 1

This book is printed on acid-free paper, and its binding
materials have been chosen for strength and durability.

Library of Congress Cataloging-in-Publication Data

Lefer, Diane.
    The circles I move in : short stories / by Diane Lefer.
    — 1st ed.
      p.   cm.
    ISBN 0-944072-41-0 :
    I. Title.
PS3562.E37385C57   1994
813'.54—dc20   94-14562
                                                  CIP

*To my father and
to the memory of my mother*

ACKNOWLEDGMENTS

"Man, Wife, and Deity" first appeared in *Playgirl*, was excerpted in *Women's Glib*, ed. Rosalind Warren, Crossing Press, and owes a debt to Ted and Harriet Gottfried.

"What She Stood For" first appeared in *The Literary Review*.

"The Circles I Move In" first appeared in *Beloit Fiction Journal*.

"La Chata" first appeared in *South Dakota Review*. It was awarded a PEN Syndicated Fiction Prize.

"Huevos" first appeared in *Redbook* and was reprinted in *If I Had a Hammer: Women's Work in Poetry, Fiction and Photographs*, Papier-Mache Press. Jacqueline Johnson, former fiction editor at *Redbook*, deserves special thanks for her vision and support.

"Vegetable Soup" first appeared in *Confrontation*, dedicated to Mariela Morales.

"The Night Life" first appeared in *Boulevard* and was reprinted in *Panurge* (U.K.).

"Wonderful Baby" first appeared in *Other Voices*.

"Huggers" first appeared in *Western Humanities Review*.

"Sophisticated Ladies" first appeared in *Sidewinder* and was awarded a PEN Syndicated Fiction Prize.

"Little Virgins" first appeared in *Virginia Quarterly Review*.

The National Endowment for the Arts and the New York Foundation for the Arts provided support during very lean years when some of these stories were written.

Contents

The Circles I Move In

Man, Wife, and Deity

My hobby is gathering evidence that Shakespeare was Jewish, or maybe black. My wife's thesis is that Homer was a woman.

I have notebooks filled with historical data, but the cornerstone of my case is the unknown rather than the known. Shakespeare was a giant of his age. How can his identity be such a mystery? There's a cover-up here, and why? In those days, everything was acceptable — illegitimacy, congenital syphilis, everything except the racial taint.

My wife, Lillian, pursues the truth just as I do, I'm sure, with the twin weapons of research and intuition, but to be honest, I don't pay much attention. When she explains, I tend to tune her out and agree with whatever she's saying. I don't mean to be patronizing, but when Lillian gets going on the subject of feminist history, she works up a head of steam. Before we know it, we're arguing about the unresolved problem between us: what I do for a living.

I write dirty books.

I write about people having sex. And sex is good, right?

Wrong, says Lillian. *It's not good. It's powerful. And that power can be used for good or evil.*

My books aren't evil. They're just nice dirty fun.

You create false images of women. You degrade us. You divest us of humanity.

Oh, come on, Lillian. It's just a living.

A fine living for a man with a teenage daughter.

Since our son is grown, married, and apparently well-adjusted, Lillian no longer cites my bad influence on him. She lowers her voice: *I worry about Cindy.*

I worry about writing enough dirty books to send her to college. A typical man, I use a wisecrack to cover my fear. Cindy is beautiful, and I know what men are capable of doing. Familiarity with Lillian and with feminism has taught me to worry all the more; I know what women are capable of, too.

What you do is harmful, says Lillian. *You're part of the system that perverts men's minds.*

How harmful can it be? I've been writing the stuff as long as we've been married — that's going on thirty years. And you know I respect you. I love you more all the time.

Probably for all the wrong reasons, says Lillian.

In no particular order, and without pretending it's an exhaustive list, I love my wife's face, her voice, her mind, her cooking. I love her high, firm principles.

Lillian and I met at a Stevenson rally in 1956. We have marched together for civil rights and to end the war. Unlike me, Lillian is still marching, still struggling to overcome. As a man, I know that the world is brutal, people are shallow, both men and women deserve worse than they get. Once upon a time, women didn't have to know all this, and it pains me to realize that Lillian, as my equal, is finding out.

Lillian works for a city agency somewhere in the wilds of Brooklyn. While I sit home and put male fantasies on paper (or, more recently, on disk), she goes forth each day to confront the world, returning at night to tell me what she has seen.

Last week, Lillian stopped at a supermarket near work to buy a container of yogurt. When the cashier refused to honor the coupon she had clipped from the Sunday *New York Times*, Lillian demanded to see the manager. The manager backed up the cashier. My wife does not ordinarily make personal phone calls on city time — *not when my salary comes out of the taxpayer's pocket*, she says — but this was a matter of principle. She phoned the executive offices of the supermarket chain. "In my middle-class neighborhood, the stores in your chain accept coupons. But here, in a neighborhood where people are struggling to make ends meet, your branch manager refuses to give discounts."

"Lady," said the man at the other end, "don't you know the evils of the capitalist system?"

On the phone, my wife sounds like a young girl. Her voice is gentle and rather breathy. There is something soothing and yet arousing about her tones. Even after all these years of marriage, her voice — its softness — never fails to have an effect on me. I once made the mistake of telling her so. "I'm disappointed," she said, those tones of hers sad and low. "So that's what turns you on. The idea of women as helpless, infantilized, incapable of self-defense like those poor female caricatures in your books, chained and tied up and available for whatever male perversion can be forced upon them."

"Oh, Lillian. These days, women only get debased in 'serious' fiction. If you read my stuff, you'd see the only whips and chains are the ones the women use on the men. The dominatrix thing is hot right now."

"I'm very disappointed in you," she said.

My wife went to work for the city five years ago because she wanted to help people. Her job title is "expediter." She is the one who walks A-1 forms through the maze of required signatures when the initiating desk cannot wait for the process to take its usual course. Without someone to "expedite," getting an A-1 approved goes about as smoothly as a Haitian's application for asylum. I wouldn't know about these things if I didn't have a working wife.

Lillian tells me she thinks the A-1's have something to do with ordering pens and pencils for city clerical workers, but she is not really sure. Her agency runs on a "need to know" basis and Lillian's department head, Mr. O'Rourke, has paternalistically determined that Lillian can efficiently carry out her functions without knowing.

From the way Lillian describes him, often and at length, Mr. O'Rourke is a petty tyrant. He vents his frustration at his undischargeable civil service employees with outbursts, venomous attacks, sudden irrational accusations. Just as inexplicably, he will turn and play the benevolent master, taking underlings to lunch at the vending machines in the basement (there being no restaurants in the wilds of Brooklyn), telling a joke or laughing at one, or authorizing the highest salary increase permitted under the emergency fiscal restraint guidelines.

About the same time Lillian got the job, she got religion. All of a sudden, she started talking about the Goddess. *Thank Goddess!* she would exclaim with heartfelt sentiment, or, when exasperated, *O, Goddess!* For several months, she went through a phase of reading the Bible at night in bed, muttering darkly. *It's the Word of God, all right, every last lie.*

The universe was created by the Goddess, says Lillian, and She is perfect in every way except for Her one fault. Like most women, she has not made the men in her life grow up.

When I was growing up, I didn't intend to become a pornographer. My wife didn't know she was going to end up a feminist. I was going to write great books, but you can't support a family on art. Lillian was always willing to work, but it turned out that on a woman's paycheck, she couldn't even support herself. Now she tells me about the Goddess. While She busies Herself with more important matters, She has allowed a lying, boastful, jealous, irrational, and generally incompetent lesser deity — i.e., God — to use the earth as a plaything. "Some little provincial satrap," says Lillian, "terrorizing his subjects when he's actually far removed from any semblance of real power. That's why he's so angry all the time. He's almost beneath cosmic notice. And that's the only reason he gets away with it."

It is clear to me, and probably to my wife as well, that her theology has been strongly influenced by years of exposure to Mr. O'Rourke.

"Accept the Goddess," she exhorts me. And here is our other great disagreement. I don't believe in either of them — goddess or god.

High principles make my wife vulnerable. She is easily depressed by commercials on TV.

"How can they?" she cries when she hears television ads. *"A German demands precision . . ."* She parrots the voice, accented and authoritarian. "It's not even the Germans I blame," she insists, always fair. "But when a commercial that resonates with Nazi values succeeds in selling cars in America . . ."

Lillian gets involved. She has volunteered to counsel rape victims at our local precinct. After her first night on duty, she came home shell-shocked, very quiet.

"What happened?" I finally dared to ask.

"I got into a contradiction with the desk sergeant."

My wife was never really a Marxist, but even now, she thinks words like *contradiction* carry radical intellectual weight. Marxist vocabulary makes my wife feel dangerous, and she insists only dangerous people are taken seriously.

People take Cher seriously, I have pointed out. *Not to mention Princess Di.*

And that, says Lillian, *is dangerous.*

"This woman came in," Lillian said, still talking very quietly. "She looked high on something. She had on a clingy dress and a lot of perfume. So the fat bastard behind the desk makes this crack — *Some rape. Looks more like a case of theft of services.*"

"And you put him in his place."

"I tried." While the sergeant persisted in believing the woman was a whore who'd called the police when she hadn't been paid, Lillian made it clear to him that not every rape victim is a fourteen-year-old virgin. "That doesn't make it any less of a crime."

"You put it very well," I told her, but Lillian was not easily consoled.

"He sent me into this horrible little room with her. *Go ahead,* he says. *Go be sensitive.*"

Once they were alone together, the victim interrupted Lillian's spiel about the counseling program and sisterly solidarity.

"Let's get this over with," she said. "The man made me go upstairs and suck his johnson."

"His what?" asked Lillian.

"Oh, shit," said the woman. "How did I get stuck with you?" Then she started screaming. "Officer! Of-fi-*sir*! How can I make a living if I gotta answer questions all night? Officer! I want a *real* cop!"

Lillian sobbed in my arms.

"Look, Lillian," I said, "you can't judge all women, or the effectiveness of the program, based on one unpleasant incident."

"You don't understand," she cried.

"Look, Lillian," I said, "it was a good experience for you. You'll understand the police business better now. . . . Next time you run into a cop with an attitude, remember what the job is like for him, always exposed to the uglier side of life . . ."

My wife pulled away from me. "I never said that poor woman was ugly."

"Of course not." I tried to restrain my male animal mind from imagining her, ripe in her clinging dress. "Prostitutes have rights," I said. "They have to make a living. They need protection, too."

"There was nothing I could do for her. Absolutely nothing," said Lillian. "She is my sister. And she hated me."

I sighed. "If you read my books, at least you'd've known what a johnson was."

Our crowd is middle aged, middle class, but politically aware. My work makes me a bit of a social embarrassment.

To make things easier for Lillian, I join her in supporting good causes.

On Christmas Eve, we went to a Fate of the Earth marathon. Lillian and I don't go out much anymore. The music's too loud, shows start too late, people drink too much. We don't have the energy we used to.

We arrived at the basement club a little before 8:00. A friend of ours was scheduled to read from her poetry and she did not get the microphone until almost midnight.

"Thank Goddess." Lillian yawned.

> *O desolate earth,*

intoned our friend,

> *purified by fire and man*
> *of each last germinating seed . . .*

She was cut short at the stroke of twelve by a large transvestite who climbed onstage and took the mike in order to sing "Happy Birthday, dear Jesus."

The poet took the interruption in stride, but the reference to patriarchal religion got Lillian going. "Is it any wonder this society is on a death trip? All this nonsense about apocalypse and Armageddon, and worship of someone who went and got himself killed . . ."

Our friend resumed reading, from the beginning.

By the time she concluded (*No raven remains to croak Nevermore*), a few inches of snow had accumulated outside, as we discovered upon making our escape.

My wife, who now recognizes that the high heels she used to wear were part of the patriarchal plot to sap women's strength, is currently partial to sandals, which she uses right through the winter, her toes protected only by tights and wool socks. The snow looked cold and wet. I hailed a cab.

"You know why paranoid schizophrenics always think they're God?" I was afraid the cabbie might answer her, but Lillian didn't give him a chance. "Because Almighty God the Father we're taught to believe in acts like a paranoid schizophrenic."

The cabbie broke his silence when he pulled up at our address. "That your building?"

Huddled on the front steps, in the snow, a young woman in a kimono was clutching her bare feet and sobbing. Lillian rushed from the cab and ran to her side.

"Merry Christmas." I tipped the cabbie well.

"You better go help your wife," he said. "Sometimes these types are dangerous."

The woman on the stoop, however, was not a psychotic stranger. She was our neighbor from downstairs.

"I'm not going back in there." She shook her head violently as Lillian knelt beside her, the toes I had tried to protect now exposed to cold and snow. "Not as long as *he's* there."

Men do terrible things to women. I was sickened at whatever it was her boyfriend had done, and at things I have done myself. The images in my dirty books are false; sometimes I'm ashamed. If this scene were pornography, I realized, a chapter in one of my books, the kimono-clad beauty in distress would have been easily consoled. My wife and I would have lured her upstairs for four pages worth of the multi-orgasmic filling of available orifices, the sensuous teasing of bodily surfaces, an older couple initiating the young innocent into every bisexual and geriatric possibility.

Instead, upstairs, I went to check on our sleeping daughter. Our neighbor sprawled on the sofa, crying and drinking our good Scotch. Lillian tried to soothe her misery by popping corn and putting some old Holly Near on the stereo.

"I can't talk about it," sobbed our neighbor. "I just can't stand it. . . . You should use nutritional yeast instead of salt." She sniffled at Lillian, one hand in the popcorn bowl. "I'll never forgive him."

Lillian gestured for me to leave the room.

The women in my books are always frank and outspoken and show no reticence in front of men. My fictional erotic men and women have no trouble relating. In real life, I understand, there are times when women can only be truly open with one another.

"I can't believe it," our neighbor was saying as I slipped into the bedroom. "I can't believe I just stood there and let it happen."

"You can't blame yourself." Lillian's soothing voice was intelligible through the wall. I longed for her. "You'll end up hurting yourself worse than he was able to hurt you," I heard her say. "What he did to you will pass; what you do to yourself is harder to repair."

"It can't be repaired. Ever."

There was silence. Lillian was probably holding the other woman, rocking her gently, maybe stroking her hair. My stomach turned as I realized how often my pen had distorted reality, transforming maternal gesture into lesbian caress. In pornography, the only comfort is sexual.

Our neighbor began to speak again, seduced by Lillian's concern. "I knew those were the wrong candlesticks. I knew it was going to drip, but I didn't try to stop him. I will never go back to that apartment." Her voice rose and she spoke slowly and distinctly, making a vow. "Never. Not as long as I have to look at those wax stains on my carpet."

It was three in the morning before Lillian joined me in bed. "I recommended a good rug cleaner," she said bitterly.

"It's the holidays." I tried to defend our neighbor. "You know a lot of people get weird . . ." I made excuses, as though by doing so I could shield my wife.

"I thought we were beyond all that." Lillian broke down completely, "How can a woman be so shallow?"

When I hold my wife and stroke her hair, I don't ask myself what instinct makes me act. "Few people manage to rise above mediocrity," I told her that night. "Male or female. It was good of you to be kind to her."

"How dare you get so superior about it?" she said. "Patriarchal society *made* her mediocre."

Anger helps Lillian banish confusion. Freed from inner conflict, she fell asleep.

For years now, I've suffered from insomnia. Not enough anger, I guess. No righteous indignation to clear the digestion. No conviction, no nobility of the oppressed. A flawed man, halfhearted exploiter of women, true lover of Lillian, writer of dirty books. When I can't sleep, I watch my dreaming wife. Her face on the pillow is so naked and exposed, so beautiful with the anger and revolutionary fervor that make women so much more interesting than men.

Pornographers aren't interested in real women, Lillian has told me. *You and your readers want a manufactured erotic image that you can create and control.*

Maybe she's right, but in our lifetime there have been changes. I can see it and I know, Lillian, that you can see it, too.

When I first started to work for the men's magazines, there were very clear rules. Breasts were OK in the photos but no nipples. You could show as much cleavage as you liked as long as the nipples got airbrushed out. The dangers of censorship: a whole generation of men grew up to get a shock on their wedding nights. *O my God, she's deformed. What are those things?*

My own marital surprise was different. When Lillian and I first met, she never went out without lipstick and rouge. After we were married, I was shocked by her pallor in the morning. A feminist, my wife no longer wears makeup. "Oh, Mom," says our daughter, "you could be practically beautiful if you'd just do something with yourself." That may be true, but Lillian's bare face stirs me more, all vulnerable and pale, reminding me of the days when we were young, just married, and I was the only man to know her true and secret face.

Obscenity laws have changed. The sex magazines have revealed secret after secret. We have shown women with nipples. Women with pubic hair. We've shown women with major and minor genitalia. For years the only thing we couldn't show was a woman with a brain.

Then, all of a sudden, the heroines of dirty books got smart. They were aggressive, independent, ambitious, successful. They took the sexual initiative and were never anybody's slave. They're better role models than anything my teenage daughter finds in mainstream magazines, in features which prepare her to buy products, please men, and covet material things.

My daughter calls women "girls," a fifties usage she's picked up from *The Village Voice*. It's not bad politics, it's "camp," nostalgia. It's "retro," and hip. I steel myself against the day my daughter will come home and call herself a "chick."

Women in dirty books don't talk like that.

"Today's market demands strong female roles," says my editor.

Does that mean feminists buy pornography? Or is it that Lillian is right: the kind of woman that women deep down want to be is actually, deep down, the type that men want, too?

Rhetorical questions. . . . I've been in this business long enough to know the market has nothing to do with the audience, and the "audience" has nothing to do with people. Someone inexplicably decides what the public wants and then gives it to them. No one offers them anything else, and so, they buy it.

So what makes it happen? The evolution of the Woman in the dirty book is as mysterious to me as the evolution of human consciousness out of one-celled beings in the swamp.

Late at night, fighting insomnia and watching Lillian sleep, it creeps up on me, the idea I can't deny. There's something behind it all, a force that shapes the market, that changes Her face. I may put Her on paper, Lillian, but I don't create Her. I don't control Her. Am I fooling myself to think it must mean something?

"Lillian . . ." How can I be a skeptic now? There's some force, whether goddess or god, that moves the Woman in the dirty book nearer perfection. "Lillian . . ." I wake her from dreams of Amazon glory and hold her, looking into her deep and sleepy eyes. "I believe, Lillian. I believe."

What She Stood For

The girls wear leather bras and panties; little electronic lights flash red and yellow where their nipples must be. This is the big production number, when they come down the runway. They look pretty ridiculous at first as they bump and grind stiffly, grimace and grin. Then, they've got it: like a batter coming into his swing, a changing voice suddenly ringing true, they connect — a sock to the pit of the stomach, a blow to the eyes. They send the boys reeling; they've blown them away, all right, right through the walls, but in fact the boys are still there, around the runway, where Ms. Rubin told them to sit. The girls can hear the whistles and catcalls, the hoots and the breathing — sharp and tense on the intake, then coming out of all those mouths in a soft low pant. The breathing wasn't rehearsed, and so it means the most, even more than the stage whisper of someone's mother in the third row: "Aren't they adorable!"

Kendra is only in the chorus and this production of *Gypsy* is just the high school show, but she's convinced: there's no business like show business. She stays out all night at the cast party. Then her mother picks her and her friend Alyssa up in the morning, because she's the kind of responsible suburban parent who knows when the kids are too drunk to drive. She kisses Kendra and her voice breaks a little as she says, "Seeing you onstage . . . I could hardly believe you used to be my little girl."

Opening night is already history. Kendra is thinking of her future. She tells her mother, "Ms. Rubin says I have a lovely bosom."

Now that rehearsals are over, Kendra and Alyssa don't bother going to school anymore. Kendra used to have to make an appointment with her shrink if she wanted to get out of classes in the middle of the day. She liked him OK, though she really had nothing to say to him. But she liked him well enough. If she ever has a serious boyfriend, she'll take him around to Dr. Weiss's office so they can meet. But now that attendance isn't taken anymore, she hasn't been to see Dr. Weiss in months. There are no more rules in school since the districts merged and black kids from the housing projects in the next town are being bused in. Mr. Gilhooley, the principal who hides in his office watching TV and perusing an old copy of *Black Rage*, is afraid that any discipline will provoke a riot, so there's no homework anymore and no tests. Kendra has heard, from the teachers, that the black kids carry weapons and most of the girls are pregnant. Maybe it's true, but while Kendra was still attending school, they all looked pretty harmless to her. Messing around all night the way she thinks they probably do and then getting up before 5:00 A.M. (because they aren't *bused* — they catch buses and make transfers and connections, sometimes as many as three), most of them fall asleep in class.

Kendra has never been on the county bus line. Her mother used to drive her everywhere, and now Alyssa has a car.

Instead of going to school, they drive downtown to the courthouse every day and hang around on the steps hoping for a glimpse of Tommy Carson, who's on trial for the serial murders of four teenage girls. If they're lucky, they see him being led up or down the steps. *Tommy!* they squeal, *Tommy!* and they wave. Lately, Kendra has upped the ante: she blows kisses.

They sit parked a lot in Alyssa's car and fix their makeup (cover-up for pimples and dark liner for their eyes), twisting the rearview mirror first to one face, then the other. They comb out their long hair, leaving strands caught in their combs, then they push their bangs back over their eyes. They talk about ordinary things: which boys they know are animals, which girls are pigs. Alyssa cleans the combs and makes a small loose ball of hair, hers dark, Kendra's light. She opens the window and flicks it off into the air, her thumb rubbing against her fingers so that, from where Kendra sits, it looks like the gesture people without it use to mean *money*.

They talk about Tommy Carson, who looks heavier and blonder in person than he does on TV (though isn't the camera supposed to make you fat?). He's from out of state and they have never actually met him or known anyone who has. What is he really like?

"No one understands him," Kendra tells Alyssa. But that doesn't mean she thinks he didn't do it. "He's guilty," she says. "He's guilty as hell. Only someone who knows that can forgive him. If I gave him my love in spite of everything, he would owe me. He would be in my debt for the rest of his life."

Kendra would rather have serious conversations with her friends than with her mother or with Dr. Weiss, and she and Alyssa do try. They talk about the threat of nuclear war and AIDS, and the challenge they will face someday of finding adequate child care while pursuing fulfilling careers. Kendra knows that all of these problems are very real and impending, but she also doubts that any of them accounts for her trouble in mind.

Back in the days when Kendra and Alyssa still went to class, they usually hung out at Ms. Rubin's after rehearsal, and now, even though they don't go to school, they still head for the teacher's house in the late afternoon.

Most of the kids love Ms. Rubin, except the ones who are jealous. She does play favorites and some kids resent her pets. But she is simply the only teacher you can trust. When Bobby Colangelo couldn't take it anymore and ran away from home, he went to Mr. Faber who had always acted very (almost too) friendly, but when he showed up with a suitcase, Mr. Faber called the police. The next time he ran, he went to Ms. Rubin and she let him move in. After Ms. Rubin started seeing Michael K. Kammerlee on a regular basis, Bobby had to sleep on the couch.

The kids watch *Oprah* and *Donahue* with Ms. Rubin — both shows, because she switches back and forth between the two with the remote control. Kendra chews on her hair, absently, but with conscious intent, just as she used to when studying, or reading, splayed out in the living-room armchair, her legs dangling over the side. Ms. Rubin doesn't believe in passive television viewing; she always tries to get a discussion going, depending on the subject of the show. If it's about incest or broken homes, she encourages the kids to talk; she also talks a lot about herself: her divorce, her troubles with men, the drugs she used when she was their age.

The kids try to help Ms. Rubin relax after her rough day. Bobby mixes drinks. They all know her speech practically by heart: "Don't be a teacher unless you want to be overworked and underpaid. And talk about stress!" She gulps the drink Bobby hands her, then says, "Give me that," and samples the one he's made for himself. "A little lighter on the Scotch next time," she says. "No, smart-ass. Not on mine, on *yours*." Ms. Rubin doesn't think minors should overdo it. "The only reason to teach is because you love it," she drones away in the direction of the TV screen. "And I do love it. It's a thankless job, but can you see me sitting around an office with a bunch of burned-out grown-ups all day? Gimme a break." The kids try to help her out. Kendra irons her dress if she's going out with Michael K. Kammerlee that night; Alyssa likes to take care of the kids from Ms. Rubin's first marriage. They're three and five and a handful when they get home from preschool and kindergarten. Especially when the beautician comes over to cellophane Ms. Rubin's hair or wrap her nails, someone has to keep the kids out of the way. Sometimes Kendra does the dishes stacked in the sink or straightens up or vacuums, hoping everyone will eventually leave and she'll be able to talk to Ms. Rubin alone.

She wants to tell her that she *did it* once with her stepbrother, when their families first merged. She didn't really want to, and now she punishes him by walking around the house in her costume from the play, but only when their parents are home and it's safe. During the day, when her mother and his father are at work, Kendra rides around with Alyssa or visits Ms. Rubin. Sometimes they drive by the house and honk and give her stepbrother a derisive wave, though Alyssa doesn't know why. Kendra imagines him in handcuffs, sometimes, led away like Tommy Carson. No one at home knows what happened, and she knows she'd end up taking the blame. Her stepfather calls her a bad influence on his little girl, Sara, but he also calls her a natural when she poses. She won't go into the basement darkroom with him when he develops the pictures. "The chemicals make my skin break out," she lies.

Now, she sits in front of the TV with Ms. Rubin, and they go over the photos her stepfather took, comparing them to layouts in *Playboy* and *Penthouse*. The shots of Kendra are every bit as good.

"Do you have a boyfriend?" Ms. Rubin asks suddenly.

Kendra's uncomfortable. She doesn't want to answer no any more than she wants to tell about her stepbrother in front of the other kids. She knows she would start to cry and then word would get around that she was the sort of girl who didn't like sex.

"You ever want privacy," says Ms. Rubin, "you know, you ever need to be alone with him, bring him here. . . ."

"He's kind of tied up these days," says Kendra, thinking of Tommy Carson.

"That's right." For the first time, Ms. Rubin looks directly at her and smiles. "Don't pressure him," she says, looking into Kendra's eyes. "Not so that he *knows* he's being pressured anyway." Ms. Rubin giggles.

Kendra's mother would die if she knew what happened, but what would upset her more is that Kendra would rather talk to Ms. Rubin. Kendra knows her mother believes in communicating and wants to be her friend. Her mom smiles shyly and waits for encouragement, but when she doesn't get it, she barges right in like Margo McCarthy at school, that leech, who needs to lose thirty pounds and doesn't even try to do anything about it. Kendra tries to ignore both of them; she doesn't want to be seen associating with either one.

Kendra's mother is a legal secretary and keeps bugging Kendra about going to college. Kendra would rather quit school and model. She tells her mother how much money she could make.

"Money's not everything," her mother reminds her. "It's not worth that much" — she snaps her fingers — "next to self-respect."

"It's the same thing," Kendra insists. "With money, you can pay your own way. You don't have to go to bed with some guy because he buys you dinner."

Her mother looks at her, shocked. "Where did you hear that? Where did you get that idea? We changed all that years ago."

Kendra looks back, shocked in return. Who's she kidding? They'd almost lost the house. Her stepfather had come along just in time. "You don't know anything!" screams Kendra. "You don't know what's going on! Wake up, why don't you! Why don't you look at the real world!"

Kendra is angry a lot and she knows she should feel grateful instead. Her mother is easy enough to handle and she never forgets how lucky she is to be an American. In South Africa, there's apartheid, which is immoral and wrong and sure to cause a bloodbath. Arab women go around shrouded in black sacks. What a horrible life! Sometimes Kendra imagines herself in prison, or homeless, or stuck in Saudi Arabia in a sack. She has fantasies about Tommy Carson. She lies on her bed or lounges in the front seat of Alyssa's car, the sunshine pouring through the windshield, and thinks what it would be like to fuck him.

Kendra and Alyssa like to drive up and park at the overlook above the reservoir. It's early spring and the leaves are hazy, a phony-looking golden yellow-green. The water ripples; it's dark and colorless, a flat unloving hue not found in any rainbow, the dull metallic match to Alyssa's steering wheel. Kendra imagines herself extended into the trees and the water; she needs more space for her insides. She feels sick. She is stuffed and clogged up but will not burst. Only boys do that. She would like to gush and then be empty. She would like to feel the relief of running clear and free, like an unstopped drain. What would it be like to explode, the way boys do? She felt nothing with her stepbrother, nothing good, that is. Even when she's found what she thinks is an orgasm with her finger, it's been nothing like that. Instead her body goes sluggish and lazy, even though her heart beats loud and fast. She feels like a hibernating beast, with everything slowed down — but she can still feel it all; she's not empty, far from it. She's too aware of herself then, stuffed up with feelings and intricate processes, languorous as though she's eaten too much, not so much peaceful as disarmed and still and — with that frantic heart — unable to sleep.

If she fucked Tommy Carson, it wouldn't be like with her stepbrother. It would be a terribly important decision. It would be a matter of life and death. Even if it only lasted five minutes, it would change her forever. It's not that she's forgotten what happened with her stepbrother, but with

Tommy, it would be different. She would consciously remember it, replaying it over and over in her mind. Her other
fantasy is to stand on the courthouse steps wearing dark
glasses and a hat that all but hides her face. Though she
doesn't believe in capital punishment, she screams *Give him
the chair! Let him fry!*

Kendra lies on her bed and cries. For a few months, whenever she felt this way, she smoked some grass or went out
and got drunk. But it's different now. She turns off the stereo
and enters the silence. She has come to love her despair.
Sometimes she bursts out crying because she can't help it,
but she has begun to set aside some time every day just to
feel bad. When she cries, she thinks about God, about extra-
terrestrials more perfect than earthlings. Kendra doesn't believe in either one. She doesn't believe in reincarnation; she's
not so sure about ESP. But her despair implies (though she
does not use these words) a possible salvation: if she had her
way, things would be different, though she cannot quite
imagine what she wants changed or how she would want
things to be.

"Nobody really listens to adolescents," says Michael K. Kammerlee. He left word for Kendra to wait for him at Ms.
Rubin's house; he wanted to talk to her. He wears a suit and
tie, a tie clasp in the shape of a gavel. If it were a little bigger
and tackier, Kendra would think he had a sense of humor,
but he's so serious, she assumes that — though he loves (or
at least sleeps with) Ms. Rubin — he's a jerk. She thinks of
him as Michael K. Kammerlee instead of Mr. Kammerlee
because that's how his name appears in the papers all
the time when he makes speeches at Zoning Commission

meetings. Since he's a lawyer, Kendra thinks of asking him if he's ever met Tommy. "It's not an easy world we've made for you," he tells her. "How are you coping with this busing business? We've certainly heard more than enough from the parents . . . but you kids are the ones who are living it. Does anyone care how *you* feel?"

So, Wednesday evening, Kendra is one of three kids sitting at the front of the room in the church basement where A.A. meets Tuesdays, Thursdays, and Saturdays. Her pastel pants are pegged tight to her legs but her top is long and loose except where a wide belt defines (as Alyssa puts in) her waist. The senior class valedictorian sits by her in a bright, loose shift. To her right, there's a big black guy wearing a T-shirt hand painted with graffiti designs that Kendra doesn't bother to decipher. There's about a hundred people crowded in the audience, and someone's brought extra folding chairs. They've moved in a podium, too, and that's where Michael K. Kammerlee stands, the moderator of this event. Kendra's mother and stepfather stayed home, at Michael K. Kammerlee's recommendation. He'd told Kendra, "I want you to be able to speak freely, to say whatever's on your mind." Alyssa is there, in the front row, grinning, with a bunch of roses she probably cut from the DeFemios' garden on the way over.

The room isn't air-conditioned, and people are fighting about opening the door and about smoking and whether there's another fan. Kendra doesn't pay attention. She's getting ready to perform, and it's not as hot in the room as it was onstage under the lights. This time, she's not just in the chorus, but she's not worried: Ms. Rubin says she knows how to hold a crowd. A lot of grown-ups get violent on the subject of busing, but Kendra has decided she will be brave and speak the truth. She'll surprise them, and be like Jesse Jackson, a nobody becoming a somebody before their very eyes. They'll be surprised at how she moves them, and someday, people will look back and remember not just this moment but how she used to spend afternoons up above the reservoir, dreamy and lost in thought.

Kendra hasn't really gotten to know any of the kids from the projects, but from what she's seen, she believes that, underneath, they are like everyone else. "We all want the same things," she will tell the audience. The main difference, as far as she can tell, is that white kids use credit cards and black kids use cash. She will tell the audience she doesn't hate the welfare kids and she isn't afraid of them. They've done nothing to her. It was easy to think out these words at home in her room; she realizes it may be harder now, embarrassing to talk about with that boy sitting right beside her. She would like him to know she hates racism, without her having to talk about it. Her mother made her watch some of *Eyes on the Prize;* she's also read *To Kill a Mockingbird* (they had to, when work still got assigned in school). She sometimes thinks she likes Victor Chin from homeroom, though she'll never let on; she'd be uncomfortable going with someone Chinese, but that's not racism. It's just because he's different — it isn't like he's black.

Michael K. Kammerlee introduces the teen panelists and asks them questions. Everyone learns that the black kid was a football star in his old inner city school (now closed), but Kendra's school already had its own team when busing started. He was counting on an athletic scholarship to go to college; now he doesn't even get to play. Sure, it's unfair, but he makes Kendra mad, thinking only of himself. There was a time when black people stood for something. The valedictorian admits (wrong verb, *happily confirms*) that she is pregnant. Having the baby will prove her sense of responsibility, she says, her mature refusal to take the easy way out. As for Kendra, Kammerlee saves her for last. He tells the audience that he's seen her at the courthouse almost every day, that he was impressed and intrigued by her interest in public affairs. He draws her out and she talks about Tommy. The audience is hushed; she's got their attention, all right.

"Neighbors," says Michael K. Kammerlee, "we came here tonight to talk about busing. And what have we found? Integration has hurt the very population it was designed to help! Even worse," he says, "more significant, and most threatening to our shared values and way of life, we have found that our anger and fear have been directed at a small side issue." He avoids looking at the panel as he uses words like *bankruptcy, vacuum, illiteracy,* and *stench,* all preceded with the adjective *moral.* Kendra feels stricken, and remembers the day her mother first gave her deodorant to use; she gave it to her wrapped up in pretty paper like a gift. Michael K. Kammerlee says the whole school board must be thrown out, top to bottom, and the responsibility for disaster must be laid squarely at the foot of City Hall.

Kendra feels naked in a way she's never felt when she showed her body; and there's nothing wrong with her body; there's nothing wrong with being naked as far as she knows. She wonders if her mother would have stood up for her if she'd come. Michael K. Kammerlee says he's running for mayor. And Kendra had expected Ms. Rubin to be there. Would her mother have said, *How dare you talk about my daughter this way?* Would she have tried to cover her? Naked now, in front of the crowd, Kendra wants to cry. She feels ashamed.

At this point, fun isn't even much fun for Kendra. She's not even impressed by the end-of-school party she and Alyssa go to at Justine's house, where they've never been invited before. Justine is rich and goes to private school, but they've met her at Ms. Rubin's, where she hangs out with her older boyfriend sometimes. For this party, Justine has invited everyone she knows.

The place could be a country club — swimming pool, tennis courts, stables, bathhouse, a private dock on the lake. Justine's mother goes around saying, "Hi, I'm Ellen Loober. Are you having a good time?" They're out on the lawn, with strolling jugglers and magicians and acrobats, with coursing clouds above in a blue sky. There's a reggae band and multiple stations for food and drink; smiling black men with white chef's hats work behind grills, turning skewers loaded with shrimp and tenderloin. The dancing won't start until dark.

"Oooohh, whaddaya think they've got over there?" Alyssa sees kids in a line. It must be something good if they're willing to wait. Alyssa has a way of slumping: her neck stretches out like a turtle's; she puts her head forward — no, not a turtle, maybe an insect extending its antennae. Kendra would tell her to stand straight and watch her posture, except that's the sort of crap parents say. Sometimes Alyssa makes her sick. And they thought it was going to be a plain, ordinary picnic. There's all these private school girls in strapless summer dresses while Kendra and Alyssa are wearing jeans.

Kids are coming off the line shrieking and waving pictures. Someone explains it's a computer fantasy booth: the woman running it takes your picture and superimposes it on a scene stored in the computer memory. What is your fantasy? Girls run by showing off photos of themselves in wedding gowns by the side of rock stars and other famous faces from TV. Boys have three or four beautiful women, all with lots of cleavage showing, hanging from their arms. One girl is in the Oval Office. Lots of kids on sailboats, lying on beaches, receiving Olympic gold medals. Brunettes turned blond. Kids standing in front of foreign sports cars, dangling the keys. As Kendra gets closer to the front, she can see the words written in gold glitter: I HAVE A DREAM.

Kendra stands in front of the computer woman, who has stars pasted on her cheekbones and glitter sprinkled over her cheeks. It's a good thing her smile is painted on because her real mouth is tight and she has the coldest eyes Kendra has ever seen. What does Kendra want? The woman waits.

What can she possibly want that will make her happy? It's not a thing you can name or see. A Gypsy walks by arm in arm with someone dressed like a fish; not far away, on the lawn, an African stilt walker takes a tumble. The computer woman is calling up possibilities on the screen. When the Royal Family appears, Kendra has to shut her eyes. Recently, on TV, she saw Queen Elizabeth standing with her hands folded in front of her, leaning forward slightly to greet someone, and she felt a flash of sickness and self-disgust. Kendra can remember herself, much younger, in a ruffled birthday dress, greeting her father in exactly the same prim way. She's not like that anymore but how would he know? Why should her father ever think about a little priss who walked around acting like the queen of England?

Kendra opens her eyes and sees her face on the screen, blipping into place in scenes with yachts, palaces. She's planting a flag on Mount Everest. She has a baby in her arms. It's cute, but how can she tell from the way it looks that it loves her? She imagines herself in a black sack, smiling and thinking, *I have a lovely bosom and no one knows it but me!* She would like to sacrifice, to consecrate her life to something greater than herself. She would like to kill Michael K. Kammerlee. She sees herself gunning him down. Then she goes to the prison and busts Tommy free. They will be on the run together. They escape to the woods. The sun goes down and the sky is blood red; they fall onto a bed of fallen leaves; she is trembling; the moon rises; an owl calls. They make love and it marks her forever and ever and when they're done, he strangles her like he did to the other girls.

"I know what you want to be," says the computer woman. "A pain in the ass. What about you?" she asks Alyssa, who's next and has her answer ready: "Fifteen pounds lighter and five foot six!"

Some people will call Kendra a tease because she gets Sean Cutler, a boy she's just met and doesn't intend to do anything with, to leave the party with her and drive up to the reservoir. (Some kids notice that when she talks to Sean about going to watch the sunset, just the two of them, she moves her shoulders so that her breasts strain and show against her shirt.)

Once at the reservoir, she ignores him. She looks out over the water and trees and pretends she is alone. She's been used and betrayed. She will never believe anything they tell her again. She will never trust anyone in this town. The sun goes down, and the sky is the same way it looked in her vision of escape with Tommy Carson, and it spills into the water, tainting and staining it, too. She knows better than to want Tommy now. Kendra is hurt and angry and, yes, she will be a pain in the ass. She will fight and reject this world with all her strength. The truth of it is, she hates them all. (Sean must see that: he's pissed off, but doesn't try to touch her.) The truth is, if she started killing, she might never stop.

This is not the sort of turning point that anyone could notice. That night, the next day, and the next, Kendra's life will go on much as before. She will fool herself that everything will be different, better, when she gets away. She'll believe that the outside world is everything the world she lives in is not and so when she leaves home she'll drop her angry caution. She will be hurt in ways that are slow and difficult of repair.

Sean, thank God, is keeping his hands to himself. She can look out at the blood red water and forget him. She imagines her brilliant future — which of course is possible, though it will be hard enough just to survive this shit, make something minor of her life but solid enough to ease her mother's worry. She doesn't know even that much won't be easy.

For now, she needs this hot secret fury. Without it, how will she ever get away? Next year, she will graduate. No one will really see her or understand. She'll put on her mortarboard and the long graduation robes and she'll walk down the runway. She will be an Arab woman, covered head to toe, her lovely bosom hidden, everything covered up for now.

The Circles I Move In

All I asked for was $5,000 to go to Betty's.

"No money," said my mother. "If you think you have a drinking problem, quit."

My mother doesn't understand you get what you pay for. "Don't you understand, this is my future," I said. "The people you recover with are yours for life. In case you didn't know it, Betty Ford alumni have weekly meetings *right here in the city*. They have *reunions*. Do you want me to make contact with the Right People, for God's sake, or do you want your daughter phoning up some three-years-sober *upholsterer* when she gets into a panic late at night?"

My mother said, "And don't call your sister either. She hasn't got money to throw away."

This is how it's always been. My father I wouldn't even ask. For Riva, it's always been low budget, cut corners, catch-as-catch-can. Is it any wonder I cannot achieve? Can anyone be surprised that I have sex with Randall?

Randall is young, but he has the instincts of a father. When he buys me an ice cream cone, he always checks the bottom to make sure it won't drip. He looks quite grown-up with his sweet Jiminy Cricket face and the three-piece suits he wears for his job behind the Xerox machine. (This is very different from my own attitude as a secretary. I say, *If you want me to dress better, give me a raise.*) Randall makes next to nothing, but he knows quality, there's no doubt about that. Both of us are waiting for something, but his idea of opportunity is different from mine. He has a knack for making something of whatever turns up — in this case, perhaps, me. He is not so much motivated as versatile, the prince of make-do. His thinking is ecologically sound, and I like it: he never expects his environment — or Riva — to change.

It was inevitable that sooner or later I would have a black friend. For some years now, I have identified with Third World countries. Here I am, full of resources which I cannot on my own — don't know how to — exploit. Downtrodden, oppressed. Fatalistic, often apathetic, but with tendencies toward internal anarchy. I haven't made much progress since leaving home.

But now I see I'm in step. America has become the Third World! Randall and I spend our lunch hours together: a bit of reefer in the plaza behind the building, a stroll up and down Fifth Avenue. Lines are too long, bank machines don't work, there's not much hope for the future. My education has gone to waste. We are appalled by the growing number of beggars, but we don't encourage them. At Trump Tower, we ride the escalators through fantasies of marble and lights, waterfalls cascading along with endless cash register tapes. Foreigners spend, while whole families from New Jersey gape and point like citizens touring Malacañang Palace after Imelda was gone.

Children love Randall. In Central Park, whole day-care center groups come running right up to his shiny shoes. He lifts little kids in his arms. He swings them till they holler. He laughs and tosses kids, like kittens, in the air.

Another advantage to hanging out with a young black man: it's easier to avoid temptation. I will *never* descend to stereotype and ask Randall to supply me with coke.

He has one fault. (But this is where our relationship becomes equal. He's done so much for me, I'm grateful there's something I can teach him.)

In the park, if a little kid does anything wrong — says a dirty word or runs off a curb — Randall changes. He starts to holler. His eyes glitter. He makes like he's going to take off his belt. Then parents and day-care workers come running; strangers interpose their own bodies and scream that violence is no solution and corporal punishment is wrong! And that's when it happens. From a self-obsessed neurotic, I'm transformed. I become a woman of experience and good sense. I have led Randall to park benches, I've sat him right down and talked to him, explaining the principles of child psychology.

"You ever have a kid?" he asks.

"I used to be one," I say, and I can tell he's weighing my words, considering these new ideas. He's going to be a perfect father someday. I'm suddenly joyful. I say, "Randall, helping someone, caring about someone, means getting well."

Our relationship is unlikely, a very strange and tender thing.

These days, it is not as easy to make friends as it used to be. Once upon a time, a simple declarative sentence was enough to start a conversation. "I have an advanced degree" or "I've just had my apartment painted" would do. Now people say, "That's nice" or "So what?" and move away.

Anyway, people don't make friends in bars anymore. They're all afraid of disease. But no one mentions the real disease, the one that runs in my family and most of the people I know: cautious distrust of natural impulse, a reliance on artificiality as a positive index of health.

I was always different. I always sought release. When I dance, for example, I let the rhythm possess me. I fling myself around without inhibition or fear and really go with it, into extremes of joy and selfless delight. What I have noticed lately, though, is while great liveliness is called for, when I dance these days, the men — the white men with my family's disease — stand back from me and watch and murmur "Incredible," and they do not mean it as a compliment.

For a long time I tried to cut men out of my life — there seemed to be no other way — but when you're a secretary, you're always bored, and so you think a lot about sex.

A secretarial job was a bad choice. It was supposed to be exactly what I needed — not too much pressure, but something to keep me occupied. My parents say I've been much too indulgent towards myself in the matter of depression and breaking down. (They also say they love me and they're concerned, but do they offer the least little amount of true help? When Randall deceives me, at least he winks. He lies without insulting my intelligence.)

I should never have taken the job. Being a secretary, in fact, turns out to be quite unhealthy. Half the time you're under heavy levels of stress and the rest of the time you sit there staring into space with nothing to do. You wish away the minutes and hours of your life — and that can't be good for you. You have lots of time to think about how you are going nowhere, and no one loves you, and it isn't ever going to change. When the boss isn't there telling you what to do and do it fast, the other voice — depression — fills in, telling it like it is. (I don't mean to imply I hear things. I do not. But I can read the writing on the wall.)

My desk is in the alcove near Marilinn's. She works for Mr. Pierce, the new black partner, and every time she comes out of his office, she practically dissolves into her chair. "Did you ever see such a gorgeous man!" Mr. Pierce is tall and curly headed and lean. He has startling green eyes and exceptional motivation. He slaps Randall on the shoulder when they pass in the hall and I understand it means nothing that he does it but might mean something if he didn't. "Even if he wanted to," whispers Marilinn, "I just *couldn't*. I wish I wasn't a racist, but I am," she says. "Can you imagine missing out on a man like that?"

"Your loss," I say, "not his."

"I would just have to say no." And she says, "You're a racist, too."

Marilinn persists in misinterpreting something I said when Randall first came to work several months ago. What I said had nothing to do with his race. The first time he came around with a stack of Xeroxing, he seemed so pleased with himself. The truth is, he's short and not much to look at, but there he was, in his three-piece suit, bopping down the hall, giving everyone a confident grin. He obviously knew something wonderful about himself that the rest of us weren't privileged to see, and so I said to Marilinn, "I bet he's got a big one."

Now I want to make it clear that Randall is not a sexual toy. He is my guiding light.

My parents would not be caught dead sitting here at Shea Stadium, flanked by Randall and Kevin, his bicycle-messenger friend. Neither would they laugh and cheer wholeheartedly, as I do. I am making a new life for myself.

I can follow baseball on TV. Live, without camera angles to tell me where to look, I get confused, so I am cheering for the hell of it, the sheer joy of it. I've recently discovered that life is competition and that losing does not give anyone a moral edge. You're in first place or you're no place! I want to win!

What I like best about baseball are player trades. You lop someone off and someone new appears. The team is still called the Mets and the crowd keeps on yelling. You replace anyone, just like that, who can't satisfy. I wish that families were more like teams.

And I love the yelling. It revs me up. I'm a very electric person — the light in my eyes, the static in my hair. In the office, people blame the carpets, but the fact is, when I touch you, there's a spark. And everything flows out of me at work. It's a constant discharge of power and that's why I need excitement, after a whole day of being a battery with a leak, losing juice.

Now I'm laughing because there's this white guy sitting in front of us with his two little sons and he just bought hot dogs and fries for all. *Mmmmm, that smell good*, says Kevin and the guy turns around and sees him — and you get the picture — he hands it over, three cardboard boats full of food.

Kevin's surprised but he still says *Thank you*. He shakes his head. *Mets fans are the nicest people!* Then he says to Randall, "What *she* laughing at?"

Randall and I smile at each other and he asks me for some money. I hand him a twenty and he calls the vendor over and gets us each a jumbo beer. He pockets the change, which is OK: he's got to show his wife some extra cash on the nights he says he's working late.

We're trailing in the bottom of the eighth and Randall knows if we lose, I'm going to be brought down. So he gives me his arm like a gentleman and says, "Come on, let's beat the crowd."

"Let's go dancing!" I say.

We know just the place. It's a midtown club where out-of-towners go to watch mixed couples hang out. We're the entertainment so we get in for free, but a pitiful glass of wine is $3.95 in this place. I pay for everything. "Here, before I spend it all . . ." I give Randall money for a cab home to the Bronx, though I know he won't be going home tonight. Is it any wonder I cannot save?

After a few drinks, I get going. I whirl around until I begin to shake, first with laughter, then with tears, until my teeth begin to chatter, and I fall to the dance floor in a heap, knowing that no one will ever pick you up until you hit bottom. I am quite aware of what I am doing, of every stage, yes, I am entirely cold and observant, but that does not mean I am calculating. Or rather, yes, I calculate, that is, I see what my acts add up to, but I come up with only the sum. I do not choose the numbers, don't you see? It is within my vision, but not my control. This is the sort of thing my parents refer

to as my *self-indulgence*. But surely I would not behave this
way if I didn't need an arm, a hand so much, and surely
someone who needs so very badly should get. And surely
they know this is serious. Certain gestures I have made or
have been forced to make were convincing enough. It seems
to me beyond question that withholding help and support
when the need is so clear is an act of intentional cruelty that
could not be sufficiently punished by centuries of torment in
the fires of Hell.

I lie panting on the dance floor and Randall says,
"Don't worry, I can handle her." He says it out loud to
Kevin, just like that. It's OK for me to hear, because I like
the thought of being *handled*. Not taken care of — that's
demeaning and can be read as a threat. But to be *handled*.
A woman who's *hard to handle*. Like a sports car. Being *handled* is OK. And his hands. He is so capable. I want him to
handle me.

Randall kneels beside me and, when I wink, he says,
"Riva, baby, come on. I'm going to take you home."

I can explain about the wink. It makes Randall feel
good to have something to offer, to be a hero, to show his
strength. He loves having the power to make me well.
But . . .

And here — I'm very clear about this — Randall agrees
with my parents and everyone else: I am not as sick as I
seem. But he *likes* that. He doesn't want to be responsible
for me, for God's sake, just the benefit of looking and
feeling that way. I wink to reassure him I'm pretending.
With that wink, I pretend I can stand on my own. He kneels
beside me, the way I want him to. He puts his arms around

me, he supports me and helps me gently, tenderly to my feet.

Randall is kind. When he comes back to my apartment, he never looks at his watch at 3:00 or 4:00 and says he has to go.

There are some people — women, mostly — who, when you tell them your problems, if they even listen, they say *How awful! How can you stand it? You poor thing!* That's the kind of sympathy, so-called, that brings you down. Randall is different. He pays attention. He *hears* what I have to say and then — there is a sort of genius in this — he *ignores* it. He grins, he winks, he touches me. He massages my temples, rubs my scalp. He puts a cold wet cloth on my forehead. He holds me close and safe, and he always stays all night.

Tonight, though, when my pills wear off, I wake and find him sitting at the foot of the bed. I say, "Randall." He doesn't turn around. He sits there staring at the television screen. Though Randall is always considerate — the sound is off — I cannot stand it. This is what I have been reduced to. He is nothing. He is no one. He is the best I can do.

Sometimes, I'm so lonely, sometimes I turn on the television just to touch it, to feel its heat, like human flesh, vibrating beneath my hand.

"I'm awake," I say. "Talk to me. I'm here."

I have told him everything about me. My problems may be trivial, but he knows my pain runs deep. I have told him about my family.

Do you see? I've asked him. Do you see how white people treat their own? Do you understand now that whatever they've done to you is the tip of the iceberg? And iceberg it is. It's cold, Randall, it's very cold. Do you see the kind of people we're talking about? Randall, Randall, I tell him, I have never had my due.

Do you know there are people in New York today who say, *I'm grateful to be an addict?* Do you know why that is? Because of the wonderful people they've met. Did you ever think of that? My mother is an ignorant woman. Betty Ford's clinic is *not* a fashionable spa. It's a very effective nonprofit treatment institution. It is *not* for celebrities only — though with some of the people you're likely to meet, it can't help but give you a boost. *Read a book,* I tell her. *Get a job!* At Betty Ford's, you are supervised *twenty-four hours a day* by some of the *best,* most *caring* doctors *in the world!* Can you imagine how that kind of attention might actually make you think you are actually worth something?

Besides which, I've told him, I was pregnant once many years ago and I was going to have an abortion. But before I could make the appointment, I miscarried, as though even God thought me incapable of reaching a decision and sticking to a plan.

"You've been good to me," I tell Randall. "I realize I usually do all the talking, but tonight I'm going to pay attention to you." I've never asked him if he knew his father, but I tell him he's lucky if he did not. "It's not what it's cracked up to be."

Randall sits there with his back to me. He's wearing sweet little peach-colored shorts. He has his head in his hands.

"But you," I say kindly, "you'll make a wonderful father someday."

"I *am* a father," he reminds me.

I hate this apartment. This *studio* apartment. I can't stand being confined in one small single room. Is it any wonder I

can't bear to clean? Without adequate closets, is it any
wonder I leave my clothes where they fall? The security
bars on the window stripe Randall's body. There must be a
moon. But can I see it? No — all you can see from this
damn window is the cross on top of the church on the
south side of the street. This might as well be a prison, or
some convent cell. I'm sure Randall expected a white girl to
have better. So did I.

"Children," I say, "will drain a man. Is that what you
want? Well, is it? I'm warning you about it. I'm trying to
protect you from all that."

Randall stares at the TV.

"They're dependent," I tell him. "Especially daughters.
They can't stand on their own two feet. . . . So what's her
name?" I ask softly. He has never told me his daughter's
name.

I get off the bed and kneel on the rug at his feet. "What's
her name?" I demand. He mouths a word and I watch his
lips. "What?"

I may do all the talking, but I am the one who's being
cheated here.

"What's her name?" I scream at him. "Say it to me. Say it
out loud!"

Randall cannot deny me, not quite, but he won't let me
have it either. He mouths syllables under his breath, like
threats.

I slip up behind him and flutter my eyelashes against
his naked back. "I'm winking," I say. He doesn't respond.
"You're too young to be a father. Too young for so much
responsibility."

He mutters something. It sounds like *thirty-eight years old.*

"She'll be OK," I tell him. "She doesn't really need you now. With girls, it's when they grow up. . . . And then, she'll get lucky, like I did. She'll find a good sweet man just like you."

He turns to me, eyes glittering, the veins jumping in his neck.

His fists are clenched now, and so I'm careful. I say, "I almost have the money. I'll be going soon. Somewhere where I can get *help. Real help.*"

His hands relax. I knew they would. "I can help you, Riva," he mumbles. "I know how to handle you."

"Yes," I say. "I know you do."

He holds me and rocks me and strokes my head. He's a prince. I'm the princess of catch-as-catch-can.

He's mine.

La Chata

La Chata's mother curses the chickens in Spanish. The rest of the time she speaks Zapotec with its Indian shushes and clicks. When she bathes, she goes behind the bamboo palisade that La Chata built in the corner of the yard. She takes off her blouse and lets down her hair. The water comes cold from the hogshead and she pours it over her body with a plastic cup. Bare breasted in the patio, she looks old.

The old man, her husband, can't see. He sits straight backed on the hard chair, his cane between his legs. When he pounds the cane on the ground, she goes to him and helps him to the hammock. In the hammock, he settles himself and draws up his knees.

The women help the men to move. At the other end of the compound, Toño's cream-colored wife helps him into the cement-block room, the only room with a bed.

The old man spits. He lifts his head to hear Marilinda's creamy giggle and Toño's gasp, a burst of air like a swimmer breaking surface.

"My daughter Chata knows how to work," he says. "My son only knew how to get married."

Inside the room, Marilinda turns on the radio. Chata bought the stereo console and built the cement-block room around it. Since no one would come to the village to put in windows, she hitched a ride down to the port, asked questions, bought glass and frames, and did it herself. When Toño and Marilinda got married, La Chata gave them the room. Then the house was more than a collection of bamboo shacks and La Chata built a brick wall around the yard and put up the iron door.

The old man knows Chata, his baby, can do anything.

Tita Carmen from across the way throws open the door that no one thinks to bolt. "Have you seen the dead man?" she asks. "They just fished him out."

There has been another drowning. It's a mystery. People have gone to swim in the river for hundreds of years and no one from the village has ever been lost. But when strangers from the refinery try to swim, they put a toe in the water and are sucked right down.

La Chata's mother mutters to hear the news. She understands more Spanish than anyone guesses. She also knows about Tita Carmen, that she goes to the city now and then and gets arrested and comes home all bloody. It's politics. She's a wild woman now.

The old man rocks in the hammock, grinning to hear Tita Carmen's voice. "Yes, there's a war coming," he says. "We're going to have another war."

The music stops and the radio announcer tells about the bomb that went off in the city, five people dead.

"*Ay, qué feo!*" cries Tita Carmen. "Who could do a thing like that?"

"You're the revolutionary!" says the old man, who should know better than to use that word out loud.

"*Ay*, but how awful! Maybe I'm not after all."

The mother thinks Tita Carmen will soon be wilder than ever. She thinks she understands. When she was a girl and her parents were killed, hadn't she been the same? How could people be that way, she'd asked. Violence was wrong. How could people kill? Why did they have to argue? Why couldn't they live in peace? It bothered her so much, it hurt, and it bothered her until she wished she had a gun and could kill them all.

"Revolutionary or not," says the old man, "you're welcome in my humble home."

"It's Chata's home," says Tita Carmen. "She built it."

Toño could have built it. He helped to build the refinery. Gave up on school and let the fields grow wild and took a salary. Once it's built, La Chata warned him, then what will you do? They'll only need people with skills. You'll have no job and we'll have lost our land.

But he took the job and bought bits of black lace for Marilinda and electric curlers to do her hair. He bought a mahogany wardrobe and a Japanese music box.

"I've been promoted to foreman," he said one day, and when he refused to fake the time sheets, they pushed him under a truck.

"Will your job be waiting for you when the cast comes off?" asked La Chata.

"My Chata!" says the old man. "When she was a girl, I didn't want her to go to school. Think of that! Now she's a modern woman, with an education and a government job, and probably she has herself a man there in town." He swings wildly in the hammock until his wife helps him back to the chair. "Well, she's old enough now. A woman of twenty-two. She has the right."

In town, La Chata eats breakfast in the marketplace, a glass of orange juice with two egg yolks floating on top. The women who squat with their baskets and tubs and children cluck to see her hurry. They are fat and imperious as ever and don't know this life won't last.

Chata takes the bus to work, to the new school the government built for the people. She waits for the director to come and unlock the gate.

Two women in the opposite doorway invite her to sit inside with them, out of the sun. Their room is like a cave. The women are embroidering together, working on the same piece of black velvet. The fabric is stretched on a frame at table height and the two women sit at either end, rolls of silk thread set up between them like a chess game. They bend over the velvet with their needles. La Chata's eyes hurt, watching the flowers unfolding in the dark.

I'll end up blind like my father, she thinks, and she wonders again what she ought to do. If she got leave from work, maybe she could drag him off to the city. It might be cataracts and they could operate. But without promising him his sight back, she'll never convince him to go. What if it isn't cataracts? It would be terrible to raise false hopes.

La Chata would like to talk it over with someone. She thinks of the director. He knows something of the world and he would listen carefully. But no, she doesn't like the way he listens, curious to learn the workings of the savage mind.

He arrives at 8:15 and she hurries across the street to join

him. When he unlocks the door, La Chata props it open with
some bricks from the street.

Inside, the patio is mercilessly sunny. There's a water tap
in the corner where the garden is supposed to grow, and by
the other wall, two filthy toilets without doors. The class-
rooms are painted a sickening green. The windows which
face the street have no panes, and the north wind blows in
dust, and the people passing by toss in garbage.

The director leaves to go to breakfast and Chata gets the
broom. She sweeps out paper, dirt, fruit rinds, and broken
glass as the children start to arrive. The girls wear short
cotton dresses that let their panties show. The boys wear
dirty little T-shirts and no shoes. Some of the children help
with the cleaning. They carry garbage out to the street.
Others cup their hands for water from the tap while some
just scream and jump around.

When the school day starts, the children go into the classroom and screech out a high-pitched song, incomprehensi-
ble and in perfect unison. They jump up and down from
their seats and run in and out of the room. The fruit vendor
stations himself at the door and La Chata doesn't care. The
children run out to buy candy and oranges, they dash to her
desk so she can approve their scribbles. The children crack
nuts and spit out shells and orange seeds to settle in the dust.
They take out pencil stubs and scraps of paper and sprawl
on the ground while they write out their vowels. Sometimes
two children will consult with each other and point at La
Chata before asking her for money.

Two nurses appear in the patio and set up folding chairs.
They vaccinated the schoolchildren months ago and now
they have been sent to immunize the rest of town. People

have been notified. The nurses sit on their folding chairs and wait.

When the children go home, there's a hot wind in the street and La Chata goes walking. There are five dark little stores in town that use loudspeakers to advertise their wares. Maybe the owners will announce that the nurses have come. She visits the stores and talks to fat, bare-chested men. Then she returns to the school.

The women in the opposite doorway call to her. The nurses are sitting and waiting, bored in the sun.

The afternoon class arrives. Children drink from the tap and splash each other and scream. Girls whisper together and take turns on the open toilets while their friends form nervous walls.

La Chata used to think education was the first step, the key. Teach the people to read, she thought. But the only books they sell in town are illustrated romances and comics. Once she wanted to study. She wanted to help children and her parents and her kid brother, Toño. And herself. Now La Chata doesn't read, except when someone hands her something political. Then she studies the ideas carefully for clues — how to move forward — and she is careful not to talk about what she reads.

At the end of the day, Chusito's panel truck is waiting outside the school. When he's traveling this route, he always stops to offer the teacher a ride as far as the highway turnoff. They head down the hill and bump along the rutted road, through the high grass outside of town, while Chusito brags about his ignorance.

When they reach the river, he slows the truck as he drives through the shallows. He opens the door, grabs a bucket from somewhere at his feet, and fills it with water.

"Radiator trouble." He rolls the *r*'s sonorously, as though announcing the winner of a race.

He leaves La Chata at the turnoff and she gets a lift in a trailer truck. Buses don't run to the village but there's always someone driving out toward the refinery that's still being built. This truck carries concrete tubes. The sun is going down and they follow the river's edge.

It's dark when La Chata leaves the truck. Now it's an hour's walk to home: the familiar path, the fireflies, wind roaring in the wild bamboo. The stars whirl and move above her like animals uncoiling in the sky, and somewhere there's a fiesta. She can hear the music pulsing through the night. It's dark now, but she knows where she's going. Here, at least, she knows the way. She can see the cross on the riverbank, marking the spot where strangers drown.

The old man is talking about modern medicine. It's a new world, full of wonders, at least for some people. His daughter Chata would know.

Toño comes out of the room. "Did you hear the radio? In the capital, everyone's gone on strike."

Everyone is silent.

Then the old man says, "Do you think La Chata is coming home tonight?" You never knew when she might get a ride. He smiles. "She drinks beer now," he says. "Two, three, or four bottles, like a man."

The mother hopes La Chata will get home. Someday she'd like to ask her about the old man's eyes, if there isn't something that can be done. But you can't have private talks in Zapotec. What you say in dialect belongs to the village, the whole village hears you, the old man would hear her talking about him. In dialect, words spread so fast, she believes they enter dreams. He would hear every word, even in his sleep.

Someday she'd like to talk to her daughter, privately, about all this politics and the trouble that's coming, but there are no words in Zapotec for some of the things she'd like to know. The mother doesn't understand about politics. She speaks no Spanish, except for curse words, and so she has no opinions.

Marilinda is looking for split ends, but even she can hear the radio going on — bombs and shootings and strikes.

The mother thinks about her daughter. La Chata never greets anyone with hugs anymore. No hearty *abrazos* for her. The mother has watched her daughter shake hands with people, cool and polite. Was that part of being modern? Or was it part of being a beautiful girl with a job? Of having to take rides in trucks with any strange man going your way?

Is La Chata happy? she wonders. What is her life like?

And she wonders, What is going to become of us?

The old man is the first to hear someone at the door. He struggles to sit up in the hammock and reaches for his cane. He slams it against the pounded earth floor.

"My Chata!" he says.

Huevos

La Estrella de Oro — The Gold Star — started out as a simple
and decent stationery store. Doña María stocked paper, pencils, rulers, a few books on religious and occult themes, and
biographies of John F. Kennedy, the good Catholic who was
certain to change things up North. She took orders for per-
sonalized Christmas cards. The proceeds weren't much to
live on, but at least her children would get their school
supplies wholesale. Doña María also lent out small sums
from the money her late husband had left her. She lived
above the store with four daughters and Consuelo, the maid.
Doña María could have easily managed the house and
kitchen — especially with four daughters to help her — but
if she didn't have a maid, customers would not take her
seriously as a businesswoman. For the same reason, Luz was
hired to assist in the store.

La Estrella de Oro had been the simple shop of a decent
widow when Luz accepted the job. She was thirteen years
old and lived with her aunt, uncle, and cousins in San Tomás
el Grande. She was a country girl.

Luz walked to the railway signal stop each day before

dawn for a twenty-minute ride to the nearest town, where she could get a bus connection to the city. From the bus terminal she walked another mile to the store. If it was raining hard and she had an extra twenty centavos, she sometimes took a city bus from the terminal, but that meant she might not have the money to take the bus at night when she was tired, and she hated to walk through the dark streets alone.

The pay was low, but Luz was satisfied enough until Doña María began to expand her horizons. She invested in an ice chest which stood at the front of the store. Early each morning, sometimes even before the metal security door had been rolled up and Luz had swept and mopped the sidewalk clean, the iceman would arrive. While Doña María had him load the chest and then paid him, Luz would hurry up the back stairs to the storeroom for a selection of sodas. After a month, they began to place orders with the ice cream vendor as well.

Luz had no objection to expanding business. She didn't mind a little extra work, and if Doña María cleared more money, there was always the possibility of a raise. The problem was that the ice-cold Coca-Colas began to attract a different kind of customer. Before, an occasional quiet student came in for a notebook, or maybe the day started with a tourist looking for a few envelopes and stamps. Now *La Estrella de Oro* became a hangout for young, teenage boys.

Doña María didn't worry. These were boys from nice families. Ruffians had better things to do than drink Coca-Cola and flirt harmlessly with shopgirls. Doña María had been thirteen once herself, but for some reason she had forgotten that, to a girl like Luz, teasing attention from the opposite sex is hardly harmless.

The most shameless was a skinny boy with glasses. Luz could sneer to herself when she was alone — the boy had an obvious need to prove his manhood; he was pathetically insecure. But when he came in and swaggered up to the counter, saying, "Nothing like a cold drink when you're hot," in a dirty kind of voice and then giggled, Luz reddened with shame. People would suspect there was something funny about her if boys felt entitled to talk to her that way. And she didn't like to hear boys giggle. Men were supposed to laugh out loud.

The ice chest was only the start. Doña María was pleased with her increased receipts and decided to go into the egg business as well.

Luz could never understand how a decent widow could have made such a decision. Doña María didn't even tell her in advance, but as soon as the egg man arrived one morning and Luz helped set up the display in the center of the store, she knew exactly what to expect.

Doña María must have known. After all, she had been a married woman. She had given birth to four children. Surely she knew more about such things than Luz did. Luz set to making the sign that Doña María requested: HUEVOS — 40 CENTAVOS. Her hand shook. *Huevos* meant "eggs," but surely Doña María had to know it also meant "testicles."

Luz stationed herself behind the counter and fixed her eyes on the floor. It would be a hard day.

The boys were delighted.

The skinny one pranced up to her. In a most refined tone of voice, punctuated by snickering from his friends, he asked, "Excuse me, miss, do you have *huevos*?"

Luz had spent the morning anticipating the question and

trying to come up with an answer. If she said yes, she would fall into the obvious trap. If she said no, the boy would pretend he was talking all along about the kind of *huevos* that were on display in the center of the store. It would be clear that Luz — not he — had a filthy mind. If she pointed to the display, she expected he would answer with a leer: "Those don't look like *huevos* to me."

"You can see for yourself" would be a clear invitation to disaster.

"Leave me alone!" would lose her the job.

"Take two — you need them" was the most tempting response, but also the most impossible for a country girl like Luz.

It was a perfect question. A perfect trap. Luz stood frozen.

"Excuse me, miss," he repeated. "Do you have *huevos*?"

Luz didn't know much about dealing with boys but she knew her job. Her sales instincts took over and the answer came naturally to her lips. "Fine hens' eggs we have, indeed," she replied, "delivered farm fresh this morning. At forty centavos each, very cheap."

The boys hooted at their friend. For a moment, Luz had won their respect.

But the skinny boy would not be outdone. He put eighty centavos on the counter and went to pick up two eggs. He returned and stood in front of her, smiling, balancing one egg in each of his cupped hands and moving his fingers. She knew what the gesture meant. It was an obscenity she accepted easily when her uncle made it, cupping his hands when he talked sarcastically of some big shot with a lot of nerve. She'd heard lots of dirty words from her uncle and learned all the gestures, but he could drink and swear without embarrassing her. He laughed out loud. He wasn't like these self-conscious boys with changing voices who focused their eyes on her chest and talked about *huevos* and giggled.

The boys played catch with the eggs until a shy one with long lashes kept one and began to pantomime. He strutted around like a woman. He played at opening a cashbox and making change. He made it clear that Luz was the model for his act.

Luz wouldn't look. She counted the money in the cash drawer again and again. The boy stroked the smooth white shell; then he punctured it at the bottom with a penknife. His mouth covered the hole and he sucked out the egg, rolling his eyes. His friends whooped.

Why did Doña María leave her down here alone?

What would people think of her?

Luz cried all the way home.

La Estrella de Oro had a fine location on Calle Independencia, only two blocks from the open market. But it was a store, a real store, and not merely a market stall. The store owners and employees along Independencia took pride in the distinction, though in many ways — and they would never admit it — they would have liked to work in the marketplace themselves. There, the women who sat amid their wares weren't separated from one another by solid walls. They shared their food and gossiped and minded one another's children.

The people on Calle Independencia were too professional for that.

All up and down the street, shopgirls stood in the doorways, reciting the bargains of the day and inviting passersby to enter. By standing that way, half in the street, they could look up and down and see all the other shopgirls. People passed, and some stopped in a store and some didn't. The patter made little difference to the customers, but it gave the employees an excuse to stand out front and gossip and inspect one another's clothes.

Luz stayed in the back of the store or behind the cashbox these days. She began to get the reputation of a snob.

"Doña María," people warned, "your girl is lazy. She doesn't do a thing to attract customers. She's always in the back. She's bad for your business."

Doña María shrugged. "Business is good." There were so many boys hanging around. They bought all their school supplies from her now and the sale of sodas was brisk. They even bought eggs, strangely enough. Surely things had not come to such a state in the middle class that mothers sent their sons out to do the marketing!

In the back of the store, Luz dreamed of escape. She couldn't get another job on Calle Independencia, not with the reputation she had. She'd heard of girls working as maids in Los Angeles, where the money was good and the work easy. All you did was push buttons, she'd heard; the actual labor was done by machine. Luz wondered how you could get a job like that, how you could cross the border. Los Angeles was probably out of reach. If she saved her money, maybe she could take the bus to Mexico City or Guadalajara, but her mother had once warned her about what could happen to a girl alone in the big city.

Luz longed for a safe way out. In time, marriage would be the obvious step. But on Independencia, Luz had no friends, and in San Tomás, all the boys had gone away to look for work. So what was an ordinary person like Luz supposed to do? It was probably better not to think about things like that.

"You'd better keep an eye on that girl of yours," people warned Doña María, "with all those fellows she's got hanging around."

And why were they hanging around? Doña María looked Luz over carefully. She was still a skinny child, still flat on top. Since the dentist had yanked two of her molars, her cheeks sagged in, and even her pretty face had lost much of its charm. Doña María knew that sometimes unattractive girls were the first to take the most fateful steps. They felt they had to. But when did Luz have the time? Well, no matter how, she attracted the boys. The boys knew how to spend.

During the windy season, Doña María liked to stay in bed late with the quilt pulled up around her. Luz had to see to the iceman and the egg man herself. She would inspect the delivery carefully. A certain amount of breakage was expected and the egg man knew how much he could get away with. At a quarter of seven, Consuelo would appear downstairs for the cracked or broken eggs, which would serve for the morning's breakfast.

After eating, Doña María's children stopped by and said good morning to Luz on their way to school. In the afternoons, after school, the girls played soccer in the storeroom. Luz had never much liked Doña María's precious offspring — they were spoiled and lazy, every one. When the soccer games began, Luz resented them even more, because this gave her something new to worry about.

The storeroom was a long passageway, built like an

interior balcony over the store. If a customer was looking for a special notebook or paper of a certain color and had trouble describing it, Luz could ring for Doña María. She or Consuelo would come downstairs and guard the cashbox while Luz ran up to the storeroom. There she would stand by the rail and hold samples up to the customer. It saved the bother of carting a large assortment up and down the stairs. More important, as soon as the customer said, "Yes, that's it," Luz could toss the article down to Doña María. The sale would be completed even before Luz had rushed down the stairs and back to her post. "That's the kind of service people have a right to expect on Independencia," Doña María would say.

And so the interior balcony was a perfect storage space. Luz, however, did not think it was a perfect soccer field. Any wild kick was liable to make the ball jump the railing and land in the store. Luz had been hit in the head once. Another time, a pile of notebooks was knocked right off the shelf. And when the ball bounced into the street, of course Luz had to run after it and toss it back to the screaming children. All this had been a nuisance, but a tolerable one. Now, with the eggs to worry about, Luz stiffened all afternoon in time to the *thwack-thwack* of the ball rebounding from the ceiling and walls. Once she had run out from behind the counter and caught the ball just before it would have landed squarely on the gleaming pyramid of fragile shells. No one thanked her or congratulated her for her quick reaction. Obviously then, what she'd done was nothing special; protecting the eggs was simply her responsibility. To Luz that meant that if the children ever did succeed with a direct hit, the cost — by now sixty centavos apiece — would be deducted from her wages.

One more burden to be borne. In spite of her growing resentment, Luz felt a concerned affection for the four girls. They would pay a price for their fun in the end and she worried about them. When they grew up, she knew what they would face for living above the store. ("Does your mother have *huevos*?") There was no limit to wickedness. Doña María's daughters were born to suffer.

In the early seventies, Mexico led the Third World. It was safe to talk about Cuba again. Doña María stopped ordering religious books and began to stock Cuban literature. For a while the store sold Che Guevara T-shirts, too, and offered local soft drinks instead of Coke.

Luz listened to the students discussing revolution and reading aloud from the newly acceptable books.

Fidel and his men had trained for a while somewhere in the state of Veracruz. Mexico, then, had firsthand involvement in the historic events. The revolutionaries hadn't been afraid of death. Prison had held no terrors. Luz heard the story of Haydée Santamaría, one of the valiant women who fought to redeem Havana from being a weekend brothel for the *yanquis*. While imprisoned by Batista, she was awakened one morning for breakfast. "Would you like some *huevos*?" asked the jailer with a smile. He lifted the cover from the platter and showed Haydée the testicles of her lover.

One Sunday shortly after mass, a new blue Volkswagen covered with fresh dust from the roads pulled up at the wooden shack where Luz lived in San Tomás el Grande. The car was followed by some curious children who had seen it at the railway crossing. They felt they'd played an important role in the drama by telling the driver where he could find Luz.

Felipe López got out.

Luz saw him from the window. Though filled with horror, she had the presence of mind to give a cousin a peso and send him down the road to bring back a bottle of Coke.

Of all her tormentors, Luz hated Felipe López the most.

Felipe was the son of the family that owned the hardware store at the corner of Independencia. He worked there behind the counter when it suited him. Most of the day he strolled. And several times a day, it suited him to stroll past *La Estrella de Oro*. Several times a day he would buy an egg, making the obscene cupping gesture with his hand. Then, in plain view out on the sidewalk, he would toss the egg in the air and let it spatter on the concrete.

Luz knew very well that few of the young men bought eggs because they really needed or wanted them. But Felipe was the only one who, right in front of her, destroyed what he bought. Luz had gone hungry at times in her life, and Felipe's ostentatious display disgusted her.

"Don't you ever get bored with this?" she asked him once, angrily.

"Yes," he had answered.

Felipe was rich and attractive. If it hadn't been for the eggs, Luz could have admired him from afar and she would never have known the truth about his ugly personality. Of course, without the eggs he never would have paid any attention to her at all, but that would have been all right. She might have enjoyed sighing over an impossible love. She would have been invisible to him forever. But under the circumstances, he had to think of her as cheap, and she was only too aware of his imperfections.

Her aunt, uncle, and cousins crowded around with smiling faces and watched Felipe drink the Coke. How had Luz managed to hook a man like this one? After all, she was twenty-six already. You stop thinking of an unmarried girl as a female at that age. You start to treat her differently. How, then, had Luz managed to lure this young man out into the barren countryside? Whatever her means or his motives, it was the chance of a lifetime.

But Luz sat silent and sullen, her humiliation masked in cold disdain. When circumstances make you look cheap, she realized, you have to be ever on guard to ward off easy assumptions. She was sure Felipe was only making fun of her. Luz had given up hoping for love. Now she stared at him, demanding respect.

The government changed hands every six years and sometimes shifted its philosophy radically. *La Estrella de Oro* kept in step but never regained its former glory. Business was slack.

When the conservative government came in, the store became a quiet place to work. There were no more lively debates. Doña María ordered rulers imprinted with the Golden Rule and disposed of the remnants of the leftist days with the telltale slogan A LINE AS STRAIGHT AS THE PEOPLE'S MARCH TO JUSTICE. She started a bookshelf devoted to the subject of unidentified flying objects and a separate shelf for books on reincarnation.

No one stopped by to torment Luz anymore. The boys had grown up and looked for more grown-up pleasures. The new little boys found new little shopgirls to tease.

Two of Doña María's daughters had babies now but no husbands. Luz was shocked, but Doña María took the mishaps in stride. "I could send them to the United States, where these things don't matter," she said. "They'd be able to get married there. But the way most men are, they won't miss anything, not having husbands."

So the daughters stayed home. Luz didn't dream about the United States anymore either. She was thirty; she was old; she had one life and one job and that was that. What was the point of running away? She had left home once to seek her fortune. She'd put on shoes and come to town to work in a shop, and it had been a mistake.

"Of course my late husband was the exception, a saint," said Doña María, "but still, I was happy enough God took him when He did. He gave me my babies, and that's all I ever wanted of that man."

Grandchildren played soccer in the storeroom. The little boys were as healthy and attractive as their mothers.

Up and down Independencia, people talked about the downfall of Doña María's girls. Luz resisted efforts to draw her into gossip about the family. Privately she had her opinion: when you shower a girl with trinkets all her life, it's no surprise she's quick to take a gift under the skirts.

Luz stood in the doorway now and called to passersby to enter. No one tried to get fresh. People on Independencia still thought she was a snob.

Luz wondered what her aunt would have said if she, Luz, had ever come home with a baby.

Mornings, after washing the sidewalk clean and filling the ice chest, Luz studied the eggs. She rearranged them in their square cardboard nests — white eggs and brown eggs in patterns, fields of color, abstract designs. Doña María had learned not to argue. It was a waste of time, but it made the girl happy; Luz wouldn't stack the layers up till she was satisfied.

Luz waited on young girls who came in running errands, and on housewives with plaid plastic shopping bags. The women were invariably polite and the servant girls had sweet, fresh faces. To them, an egg was an egg.

Luz rang up the purchases. The eggs were clean and shiny and innocent. They were nutritious and cheap. Who could have guessed that this simple job and these graceful, fragile shells could turn a life from its expected course?

Luz never walked from the bus anymore. She was too tired.

In San Tomás el Grande, Luz had taken to telling stories. Before she had come to live with her relations, she said, she had been at a plantation in the state of Veracruz, where her mother had worked as a cook. One day a group of Cubans had come, looking for room and board.

"They said they were from Jalisco, but we could tell they were Cubans," she explained, "because they said *chico* in between whatever they were saying. It was always *chico* this or *chico* that." Her listeners would laugh and nod their heads in recognition; they had seen Cuban characters in movies so they knew the idiosyncrasies of Cuban speech. They had heard comics talk with Cuban accents, just as Luz had.

"I was only a child, and sometimes I followed them out into the hills. Imagine my surprise! Do you know what they were doing there? They had guns and rifles and they crawled around on their bellies. They ran and jumped hurdles and climbed over fences." She would close her eyes, as if remembering.

"The one with the beard pulled my braids once. I was only a child, remember. *Never tell anyone what you've seen or we'll have to shoot you,* he said. He said it like a joke, but even though I was a child, I knew this was serious business.

"Juan was the name of the black one. He was the friendliest. He would sing to me and play with me.

"There was a woman, too. Her name was Haydée and I think she was the bravest person I ever met."

Luz wondered when it was that Fidel and his men had trained in the Mexican countryside. Had she even been born then? Who cared?

In San Tomás el Grande, they began to call her *comrade*. They pointed her out with respect as the woman who had fought alongside Fidel. Some said she had never married and never would because of something that had happened back then. Batista's men were dirty pigs. "They served them to her on a plate" went the story. "Can you imagine?"

Luz didn't mind what they said. She knew people have to whisper something about a woman who has no man. Still, she hastened to set the record straight. "No, no, I never fought by his side," she said. "He was only a friend of mine, and I was very young."

But how the mighty had fallen! She had stood by Fidel's side and now she was nothing but a wage slave. In the city, Doña María talked proudly of the shopgirl's loyalty. Aside from some adjustment for inflation, she hadn't given Luz a real raise in years, yet Luz had turned down several other offers. Some people don't know what to make of their opportunities, thought Doña María.

Luz washed the sidewalk clean in the morning; she locked up at night.

Each day brought the torture of anticipation. Luz would hear the kick and the children shouting. There were six grandchildren now. The ball would bounce and rebound and slam and crash, and a chill would slowly move up the shopgirl's spine. When the ball flew over the rail, she held her breath. It would hit the floor and roll behind the counter or into the street. The children would laugh with relief.

Behind the counter, Luz clenched her fists and waited. The ball couldn't miss forever.

Vegetable Soup

Her mother, her sisters and their children, her brothers —
they all greeted Dominga, but her father made her wait. He
didn't look at her, just studied that newspaper he has —
a couple of yellowed pages that came wrapped around
some wool he bought in the valley I don't know when. He
sat there, taking his time. He made her wait and when he
raised his eyes, I guess he saw right away she'd lost her
braids, but he decided to let it go. He nodded to welcome
her home.

Illiterate old man, she must have thought, old fool. At least
this time he wasn't going to hit her. With his old piece of
paper, he was letting her know he wanted to be considered a
modern, educated man. He wouldn't put up a fight over her
work as long as she let him have his pride.

"Father," she said, with respect.

That was Dominga's homecoming as I see it. I can't see
through walls, but I know my neighbors.

Dominga got to work. The cement floor she'd laid down
in the hut, must be two years ago, was buried under soft
dirt. Her family watched as she swept. Then she stood in

the doorway looking at the mountains, seeing things. In time, there would be neat square homes made of brick, with cement floors and with the animals kept outside. She imagined squash would grow green and yellow and sometimes silvered with the mists. We have mists and a chilly fog here in the mountains. Only high up on the ridge would you still spot stalks of tough blue corn. Up here with the blue corn, that's where I am. I wave to her, but she doesn't notice. Dominga's vision is so broad now, an old man like me tends to get lost. But I know what I know. I can figure where it started, though I sure didn't see where it would end.

"Did you stop at the mission?" her mother asks. "How were the sisters, and that nice young priest?"

And I see Dominga lose her confidence. Why did her mother have to mention that priest? "He wanders on the cliffs howling at the moon," she says. Up here, that's what happens when you try to help. "The sisters pray and tell the orphans to cover their ears."

Dominga's mother crosses herself and blows into her fist.

"It's not the Devil!" Dominga says. "It's malnutrition! That good, kind man has lost his mind."

No one speaks for a moment. Then Dominga's mother asks the question that has been worrying her almost all the time her daughter's been gone: "You haven't turned against the Church, then?"

"No. Why would I do that? Those Church people care about us."

"Then the other one isn't working with you?"

"What other one?"

"The one who teaches school."

That's a surprise to Dominga, all right. She hadn't known about Santiago.

Her father knows all about Santiago. He spits to get his daughter's attention. "He's a Communist. That's what he is." He hisses the word between his teeth. "Yes, modern times have finally come to Miahuaxtla. The Communists have discovered us. The Evangelists and Mormons will be next."

"But *I'm* supposed to teach school here," Dominga says.

"Modern times." Her father's voice cracks as he laughs. "Yesterday, not a soul could read. Tomorrow we'll have two schools to choose from."

We're traditional people here, which is supposed to mean we don't like to change much. If you know us, they say, you can predict us. And I know us. I don't have to be there to know what people will say or do. Up to a certain point, of course. The way I tell it may not be exactly all the time the way it happened, but I can give a good account. Up to that certain point, maybe past it.

I watch as Dominga comes out and sits in the dirt, her legs sticking straight out of her short city skirt, her back against the adobe wall. I want to tell her, put a blanket on. At least a shawl for your head. Child of the future, you're going to freeze in nothing but that skirt and sweater. But she's too busy thinking to hear me. Whoever the Communist is, he's an outsider. That won't help him here, she thinks. He probably doesn't even speak a word of Mixe. He won't get far with nothing but Spanish. Dominga looks at the mountains and I wave again.

That's how I see it. Dominga was one of ours, a good child, though I didn't like the way her eyes surveyed the village.

We're all good people here. Her father, too, and if he hit her, well, isn't a father allowed to? What was he to think when she came back from that school before, her coming and going at all hours of the day and night? Not an open-minded man, but intelligent. Illiterate? Well, so am I. I never had any difficulties with Dominga's father, nor he with me.

In the morning, Dominga made the rounds of the village. I can see Carlos Reyes cutting his breakfast short to meet her at the municipal building. A fine year he picked to be municipal president, poor man. He takes off his hat. He stands up straight behind his table, in front of the government photographs and the flag. He drones his speech at Dominga, staring straight ahead like a soldier. Never once looks at that girl's face. "On behalf of the entire village and our patron, San Isidro, welcome back to Miahuaxtla." I've heard it all before and don't have to be there. "My neighbors have chosen me for this post, to carry this burden of great responsibility. . . . I welcome you back as a daughter of this little place in the world, but I also welcome your help in bringing Progress to Miahuaxtla. You can count, of course, on my full support."

I know Dominga knows better than to believe him. She thanks him and goes on her way, through streets muddy from the morning rain. She's going to visit everyone this morning.

In the Sánchez yard, Doña Chepi hands her a clay bowl filled with *atole*. That's our drink. You get it from the corn, the cornstarch all beaten up with hot milk. You got to jiggle that bowl while you drink it so it doesn't turn to glue, but Dominga's holding it like she's forgotten how. Jiggle that bowl, I want to tell her. People are going to say you're too good for us, used to drinking Nescafé. She jiggles it. Then she eats a tortilla filled with warm black beans. She isn't hungry, but she won't get anywhere if she refuses what people offer. And the *atole* and the tortillas hot off the fire keep her hands from hurting in the morning frost. She's not used to our climate anymore.

I'll bet our homes look small and dark to her now. And empty. What have we got? Some sacks and covered baskets, bundles all rolled up. A shirt, a hat hanging from nails. Someone's got a new plastic bag with a handle. Someone's got a bench and a bucket and a picture of our saint set out with candles for him and some plastic flowers.

"Some people go away and study and never come back," she says. "That's not why I went. They think maybe they can have a better life in the city. I think I can't have any kind of better life unless I can have it here in Miahuaxtla, here in my home."

"But this is a poor humble village. . . ." That's what Panfilito Sánchez says, and she hears it again and again, as she goes from house to house. In yard after yard, she jiggles more *atole,* she eats more tortillas and wonders if the people have saved anything for themselves, if there will be food for the children when she leaves.

"It's because I love this place and the people who live in it that I studied to be a *promotora,*" she says. "That's what I'm called — *promotora*. Because I'm not just a teacher or a nurse or a seamstress, though I've learned how to do all those things. I'm a *promotora,* because that really explains why I have returned — to promote. To promote our standard of living and our quality of life to higher levels, to move forward, to promote Progress." Her eyes shine, her brown cheeks flush warm.

"Progress is important, señorita. Everyone in Miahuaxtla agrees with you. Why just the other day, our municipal president was saying . . ."

It all goes the same way in hut after hut, more sacks, more tortillas, more words, more saints, except that as the sun rises, the mud dries and then the flies and chickens stir up the dust. No one mentions Dominga's last time home, almost two years ago, when she made the same visits and everyone said the same things and then ignored her. That time, she got sad and so discouraged she disappeared again, back to the city to study some more. I want to tell her it's not worth it, what she's doing. Unless she's doing it for me. I'm happy enough alone on the ridge with my dogs, but I still enjoy watching things that happen. Traditional or not, I like to see something new. An old man still has his curiosity.

"You've seen the washstand I built for my mother," Dominga tells Altagracia Miramontes, "and the hearth for cooking. I didn't build them to make people say, *Oh, look at that Dominga. She thinks she's better than we are.* I built them because they've made my mother's life easier. She doesn't have to carry the clothes down to the river anymore. She doesn't have to kneel on the rocks and scrub all morning and carry everything back and forth. My mother's too tired to bend so much. You know my mother doesn't give herself airs — but the *lavadero* has made her life easier, better."

Dominga clears her throat. The dust is terrible.

"I built my mother a *fogón* — a cooking hearth — in a separate shack beside the house. She doesn't have to kneel in the dirt when she grinds the corn and cooks. And the fire burns safely on the hearth. Our house won't burn down around us while we're asleep some windy night."

People nod with approval. "Yes, señorita, yes. You're right. When we cook and eat on the ground with the animals, we expose ourselves to microbes, to disease."

"Would you like me to help you build *lavaderos* and *fogones*?"

"Of course, of course," people say. "We believe in Progress. A *lavadero* means Progress. A *fogón* means Progress. You must have many people to visit. We won't keep you here any longer."

So far this is what she expected. So she'll give each family a gift of vegetable seeds and they'll throw them to the chickens once she leaves. Words, only words. Except there's something strange about the words. How long will it take her to catch on? Will it occur to her in the fourth hut, or the fifth? How long? She'll stand a moment in the doorway: "How do you know about microbes?" she'll ask. "I never said anything about microbes."

"Santiago told us."

I used to meet with Santiago in the mornings. Actually, the children used to meet with him. I sat just outside their circle. Sometimes a few of my dogs would follow me down from the ridge and we'd watch him scratch symbols in the earth with a stick.

One day after Dominga's return, it was a matter of time, someone — her youngest brother, or maybe Amalia Bautista, the old gossip — had to lead our *promotora* through the ravines so she could get a look.

"Where did he come from?"

"Who knows?" her brother answers. "One day he was here. He was sick and his clothes were in rags. People took care of him and fed him. Women wove new clothing for him to wear."

"He's a beggar!" she exclaims.

"No, no, he just needed our help. When he got better, he said he wanted to repay us. But he had no money, he had no land. Finally he said he would repay us the only way he knew how. He would teach us to read and write."

I'll tell you something about the people of Miahuaxtla. I've heard us called closed-minded and ignorant and cold and cruel, but we're quick enough to help someone in need. People who've passed through here — the priest who comes now and then, the anthropologists, geologists, all the -ologists — well, they haven't seemed to like it much, but they're always sad, or so they say, when it's time to leave.

Imagine it. They walk on in silence, and Dominga stumbles once or twice. She has become accustomed to paved streets.

"He's nice," says her brother. "Very simple. Like Che."

After years in the city, I figure Dominga's heard about Che, but she wonders what her brother could know of a revolutionary like that.

"What is *che*?" she asks, pretending.

"Not what. *Who*." Her brother laughs because he's happy to know more than this modern girl. "Che was a simple man," he says. "Che lived with the humble people the same as they did. We all love Che very much."

"Is that all you know about him?" she asks.

"What more is there to know? He was a man of great *cariño*, of great love and affection for the people."

For a moment, Dominga would like to give up and leave it all behind; she wants to break into a run. But you can't run through the ravine, certainly not in city shoes. How had this Communist, this outsider, won so many hearts? *Cariño* means more than politics, she tells herself. Remember that, she thinks. Love them. But in the meantime, the blood tingles in her fingertips and her hands are stinging, on fire. Can she turn that fire to *cariño*? "Che was not as *cariñoso* in life as he seems to be in death," she tells her brother sharply.

They climb the ridge and the boy squats, then points to the clearing below. "There he is. There . . ."

Santiago, the Communist, squats too, on the ground before a straw shack. He scratches out letters in the dirt before a few unwashed children and one old man who sits to the side. Dominga almost laughs with relief. I'll do better, she thinks. I'll reach all the people. Now she does laugh because at school and in church they had told her so many times that Communists were evil people, powerful people to be afraid of. But that small man in a denim jacket, that Santiago squatting in the dirt, is proof that even Communism can't break through the stubborn closed-mindedness of her people. A few dirty children and old Ignacio, the crazy man. My ignorant, thickheaded neighbors, she thinks, loving us all.

When they call me crazy, I think it's with affection. I've never done or said anything out of my senses. True, I went off to fight the Revolution with the Zapatistas, a fairly crazy thing to do. People from San Isidro Miahuaxtla usually know better than to get involved. I guess I found out they're right. But all that was — must be — sixty years ago. Now I keep mostly to myself and don't give trouble. Old crazy man. It's an honorary title.

Dominga gives up on the grown-ups — too set in their ways — and starts meeting with the people her own age. But our young people don't find her as interesting as they expected. The girls want her to cut and curl their hair. They all want to hear stories about the world away from here, but Dominga's put on a long blue skirt same as her mother and her sisters, and her thoughts all revolve around Miahuaxtla now. Her other mistake — instead of talking about the city, she talks about herself.

"Do you remember the last time I came back? I was so scared, I was shaking and trembling all the way home. This time, I know it won't be easy, but I know what to expect and I'm not afraid."

Now I'm not blaming her. If she hadn't thought a lot of herself to begin with, she'd never have thought to leave home. I was that way when I was young. When I look at Dominga, I wonder how it would have been if I could have left this mountain to go to school instead of to war. The same I guess. You come back and people say you've changed. People say you don't belong here now. And when no one understands you, it's natural to reflect on yourself, on and on. But here in Miahuaxtla, we call that kind of thinking selfish. I bet that's what people say about Dominga now.

The young people are quiet. No speeches about Progress and moving forward. Maybe they are listening, or thinking.

"You went to school before," one boy says at last. "Wasn't that enough? Why did you go again?"

I thought she would tell him the truth, about how her

spirit failed her. She had to run away from us for a while, back to the praise and the encouraging teachers and three meals a day, the clean-smelling toilets. Showers — that's a good way to wash clean — though I bet they don't heat the water for *us*, even when we're civilized like Dominga.

"I've learned a lot more," she answers in a hurry. "I've learned about rabies."

Without going to school, I know all about rabies. I've used this machete to put a few men out of their pain. And once a little girl, which was terrible, something I didn't like to do. But a rabies death is too hard and ugly.

"I've brought serum," she says. "If you'll all help me gather the village dogs, we can inject them. Good prevention," she insists. "With your help . . ."

When she mentions help, the group — naturally enough — disperses.

"Do you know what else I learned?" she whispers after they go. "On this earth you can't do things without suffering. That's the way it is on this earth."

I heard that, Dominga. You stood alone in the plaza. There were lizards running at your feet and vultures circling overhead, and I remembered back to when you were a child. You had sores on your face like all the other children, and urine — just like them — trickling down your skinny legs. You were no different from the others then.

We were taught not to set ourselves apart, you remember. No more talk of suffering. Don't ask me, child, for pity.

Look, Dominga, look! The latrines you built two years ago stand ready in a row. They don't stink. Why not? Because no one uses them. People go the same as always — anywhere between the backyard and Oaxaca. Does that make you a failure?

I'm a citizen, you remember, one of them. That's all.

There's nothing to be ashamed of, Dominga. Why do you care so much about these things? What does it matter? It makes no difference. You can make no difference. Don't you know?

Weeks go by. Dominga hasn't been around to visit or lecture or badger. People start to talk, to wonder. Maybe she's sick. People start to drop by her family's house.

"I've been busy," she explains. She's made an open-air classroom beneath a thatched overhang. She's built benches and long tables to use for desks. She shows off her newly planted vegetable patch and explains about squash and radishes and carrots. She says, "A school must have a kitchen," and makes everyone go look at her *fogón*. It's away from the house, on the other side of the yard.

People shake their heads. She wasn't sick after all.

Considering all I've said about us, you may be surprised to know that Dominga's school was only in operation one week when the morning class grew so big many students had to sit on the ground. At night, men came to study by torch and candlelight after they finished work in the fields.

Dominga talks and talks — one day about Health and Nutrition, one day about Rural Hygiene, new words to go along with Progress. She passes out handfuls of little perfectly formed letters and we arrange them the way she likes. She passes out paper and pencils and we copy the shapes. When class is almost over, she moves gracefully among us and checks our work. Her voice is soft and gentle when she is pleased. She gathers up the letters, her secret weapons. When they've been poorly copied or placed wrong, she shakes her head with its short curled hair. She tosses the pieces back into her burlap sack. But the letters that line up the way she likes them, from A to Z, those she scoops up and throws into the big pot bubbling away over the fire of the new *fogón*. The alphabets swim along with potatoes, squash, and carrots, a little salt and garlic, a bit of chile.

The people of Miahuaxtla are hungry for knowledge. We wait to be served, knowing we've made Dominga proud.

It was about this time that Santiago left the village. He had to visit his family, he said. There were stories, however. Some people said he was headed even higher into the sierra to meet with his comrades. And there was talk about a soldier-woman called Lina and some people said she was a nun.

"Yes, she's notorious, that Lina," Dominga told her night class. "Everyone in the city knows about her. She left the Church, or rather was asked to leave, for, well, for sexual reasons, let's say. She found an interest in Communism later. Because of the free love." I don't know if our Dominga really meant to lie. She just put into words what everyone was thinking. But when she said it, that made a difference. She put her authority behind the kinds of dirty things people naturally like to talk about.

Not that it hurt Santiago any. When he returned, his personal affairs were soon forgotten in the excitement over arithmetic. I'm not stupid, but I'd never learned to count past five before. Anything more than five, well, I called it a lot. What difference did it make? There were many others like me. But Santiago showed us what the difference was and he made it easy too when he brought us black beans to use as markers. I like multiplication best. The numbers get so high so fast, so many beans end up in the pot!

They transformed us. Miahuaxtla was transformed. I've lived through hundreds of tremors and four terrible quakes, but our place in the mountains was never so shaken before.

Men and women ran from one teacher to the other. No time left to drink too much or get into fights. Dominga was busy on one side of town, Santiago on the other, installing those famous *lavaderos* and *fogones*. When they want you to have one, how can a regular student say no?

Mule trains wind up the mountains carrying mattresses. Men jog along, bent double under heavy loads, tumplines across their foreheads to help them balance sacks of potatoes and onions and beans on their backs. Dominga builds wooden platforms to use as daytime tables, nighttime beds. But she's not blind or stupid and neither is Santiago. They must see, as I do, that the *fogones* are soon dismantled and families save the piles of stones for more useful, though still unknown, purposes. Do they see Amalia Bautista casting proud eyes over her new modern mattress on the table before unrolling her straw mat and going happily to sleep in the dirt?

"It's not healthy to have your livestock sleep in the house with you," Dominga says. Everyone agrees wholeheartedly. You can't consider a pig (if you're lucky) and a scraggly hen livestock.

I ought to say, by the way, I've never been in Amalia Bautista's presence when she unrolls her *petate* and goes to sleep. To keep matters clear . . . Amalia Bautista spreads gossip. She doesn't, alas, give rise to any.

It was Amalia Bautista who noticed we were becoming

spoiled children. She went to Dominga and asked for a *lava-dero*. Dominga said yes, of course, if you'll let me build you a *fogón* first, and if you really use it, too. Amalia Bautista smiles her half-toothless smile. "When Mama says no, run to Papa." Santiago built her a *lavadero* and set no conditions. Well, why should he? Amalia Bautista took care of her younger brothers and sisters since she was four years old. Life was always hard for her. Now, why not let her have her way?

For some time, I'd been sampling Santiago's beans during the daytime classes. Then I would drop by Dominga's for a bowl of soup at night. Who could begrudge an old man a little something? But when other students started to follow my lead, Santiago laid down the law: "It's her or me."

In the end, we all promised to stick with Santiago. Then we hurried to Dominga after his class. We told her he was being unreasonable. With so much to learn, why shouldn't we attend both schools? We said, Santiago doesn't have to know. Let us continue studying with you at night — but in secret.

Dominga listened, then stood firm. "If we are to be free, if we are to progress, we must learn to make choices. Choose," she said.

The other students seemed to understand this but I, reputed not to be in possession of my faculties, could not. "Will you send me back to my shack, with a taste of learning and a growling stomach?"

"Education is for everyone," said Dominga, "but under the circumstances, I have to say you are no longer welcome here."

Choose. This was one point on which Dominga and Santiago agreed.

So I'm still up here growing my Indian corn, the kernels black, blue, and purple, tough as the soles of my bare feet.

I watch Dominga's visions come true. They've started to collect and burn the garbage in the village. The beds go unused, but there are cement floors to sleep on instead of mud. Sometimes the floors get swept clean.

A grand success . . . but . . . I wonder. What does Dominga think when she weeds the vegetable gardens? Her little patches thrive, but she'll never grow enough to feed all the hungry. Besides, in the gardens, that's where you see so clearly those boundary lines. Dominga's friends plant corn and beans and chile and carrots and squash. Squash. That was the great gift she brought us from the city. Santiago, on the other hand . . . well, what kind of romantic tryst is there with that soldier-woman, Lina, when he returns bearing his own sack of alphabet noodles and cabbage seed?

"Yes, I guess all vegetables are good for you," Dominga admits. "It's just that I've always found that cabbage carries parasites."

And when Santiago had a fair-skinned visitor, a *huero*, a white man, the whispers spread through town. "He has hair the color of corn silk, eyes like the sky." I guess I would have thought he was frightening myself if I hadn't met a few on my travels. People went to consult Dominga. "Do you think *hueros* are human?" I'll bet you anything she met a few in the city and probably saw them in the movies, too. But she knit her jet black eyebrows and said, "Who knows?"

I didn't much like the way she was behaving, but still I

favored Dominga in the struggle. One of our own — though some people began to doubt it. But Santiago, I've got to hand it to him. His students learned real big Spanish words with their alphabet noodles, words like *campesino* and *proletariado*. Amalia Bautista, bless her, was delighted as ever. "I always thought I was a Mixe," she exclaimed. "A Mixe Indian. Come to find out I've been a peasant all this time!"

Santiago didn't play fair either. "Are you going to listen to a girl?" he asked the village men. That's when he gave me the idea. When he asked, "Since when does an old maid tell you what to do?"

Yes, so I lied. I sent down word that I was dying. That brought the both of them running, climbing up my ridge with their medicines. I never before knew I was worth so much, the two of them each so anxious to be the one to save me.

"It's my pressure," I said. "Shooting way up." They looked at me with suspicion. "My stomach," I said. "The gorge, the bile" — and this was true — "it's always rising." They looked at me without trust, the crazy man. They made me sick, the two of them, and in truth I felt very very bad. I said, "Both of you, you together, you can cure me."

I said, "Get married."

That was my idea, but the words came out so fast they took even me by surprise. I hadn't planned to get to the matter so quickly. "Really, my boy, she's not bad looking, and who here will have her? How old are you, girl? Nineteen, twenty? Her sisters were married as soon as they were old enough to bear a child. Who else in this town is smart enough for her, modern enough? And you, Santiago. You know they'll never let you teach their daughters as long as you're single, not with the reputation you've got."

Dominga started for the door.

"Don't go!" I said. My pressure did go up then, and my anger. "Stay! Listen to me, both of you. Do you think I care whether you kiss and embrace and hold each other close all night? That doesn't matter to me. That's up to you. A man and a woman. You'll find all that out for yourselves. That's not why I say to get married. I want you together because we are one people. Why do you make us choose? You offer your soup and your beans, with a little salt, a little chile, a little hate."

"No!" I got Dominga's blood rising, too. "I came back to Miahuaxtla out of love. This is my home. These are my people. It is done with *cariño*, with love."

I laughed so loud, it set the dogs howling.

Santiago interrupted. "They say you rode with Zapata," he said.

"Yes, I was a Zapatista." To tell the truth, I started out just fighting, but Zapata's was the side I ended up on, for all the difference it made. I joined the Revolution, for justice, for my rights. For the good land they took from us so long ago I wonder sometimes if that good land wasn't just a story. I fought to be part of a nation, to be part of a movement. I was part of it, with my rags and my lice, until so much wanting to be part of it left me wanting to be left up here alone. I started remembering things and then Santiago asked that question: "What did you fight for?" he asked.

It just happened: I had his hair in my hand and one fist under his chin. As though that was my answer, that a blow is a reason, that a man can't expect good sense.

When I went down the mountain to fight, I saw so many things. Railroads and towns, mirrors, window glass. Corpses piled like firewood. Blood and fire. I saw people reading newspapers. I saw pigs eating their way through dead men's flesh. Does it take killing to open a man's eyes? Did I need to go to war for this, telegraph lines, electric street lights — all the things we'd never seen in Miahuaxtla. I'd never even thought about those things.

What did I fight for?

I hit Santiago again. I never meant to hurt him. I thought, I don't want to fight you. I don't want you fighting each other. Haven't we got enough to fight? I'm telling you the truth, I felt a great remorse and I still feel it. But it was my rage and I couldn't help it. I never had the chance to become a civilized man.

Santiago didn't fight back. He knows you don't hit an old crazy person. He picked himself up to leave. Dominga was already gone.

But ideas. I told them my idea and you see what can happen with ideas. Maybe it was that night, maybe later, after Dominga had her own house, two rooms, very nice and made of brick. Her father didn't beat her, but he didn't want her under his roof, either. At night, the wind howled, but Dominga wasn't afraid of ghosts or wandering souls. Her mattress was firm and comfortable and her roof kept out the rain. There were no lice in her blankets. But still, at night, sometimes, Dominga couldn't sleep.

"Dominga, will you let me in?"

See, it was just as well she couldn't sleep. There was always an emergency, a woman giving birth, a child with fever.

There was a night when Santiago must have appeared and said, "I've been thinking about old Ignacio's advice."

I imagine Dominga was shocked, hearing words like that from him at night as she rose from her bed.

"Don't be afraid," he said. "It's not what you think. . . . I came at night so no one will know about our meeting. I do think there are ways we can cooperate."

Dominga said nothing to encourage him. But she sat and listened.

My dogs went wild and chased off to march with the little girls. The girls had never marched before, except for practice, but they would have giggled and lowered their eyes, I think, even with more experience. Each wore a dress, in green or red, and each a white pinafore with our national symbol traced on. There hadn't been time to embroider. They marched two by two down our narrow village paths, then spread out in chevrons and spirals as they moved into the plaza, stopping before the church to be blessed by the visiting priest.

The girls in green carried paper flowers. The girls in red carried butterflies cut from bright yellow paper and as they marched, their skinny brown arms floated upward and together, making the yellow butterflies drift and meet.

The aroma of barbecue floated over Miahuaxtla. A man asked "What is that smell?" "Meat," his wife replied. He shook his head. "Ah, I had forgotten."

You may ask, What was the occasion? Dominga had decided that Miahuaxtla should help the President of the Republic celebrate his saint's day. And well he might need help. Church and State are separate in our beloved republic.

If the President cannot honor his own saint, it is an honor for us to do it for him.

The church bells rang. It was a glorious day, which made us glad because so many visitors were in town, come to enjoy the fiesta, standing there in the plaza with Santiago. In front of strangers, of course the village put on its most enthusiastic, patriotic air. "*Viva el señor presidente!*" shouted Amalia Bautista, using his title because she didn't know his name. Men stepped forward, urged on by Dominga, and moved through the shuffling steps of traditional dance.

Santiago's companions looked grave and so did he, but I think in fact he could hardly hide his satisfaction. "The government has bought their loyalty with fiestas and food," he said. "Don't expect me to win them over if I have nothing to give."

He yelled at the shuffling men to stop their dancing. They gladly obeyed. Anyone can dance, but it's an occasion when you get to hear a good speech and it sure looked like Santiago was going to make one.

"The government talks about the native people," he says. "The government loves us. The government wants to protect us and help us," he shouts. "But let's look at the truth. The white men in the North have a saying: *The only good Indian is a dead Indian*. The powerful men in the Mexican nation have a saying, too: *The only good Indian is on display in a museum*."

A crowd gathers in front of the latrines to nod and drink and listen.

"We aren't people. We're folklore. Isn't that the truth? We have to be protected so that we can be colorful. But are our rights protected? Our lives? They talk to you of Progress and offer you the rights of a dog. They say your culture is a national resource, like our oil, our silver, our gold. Well, have you seen the mountains after they go in looking for silver? Have you seen the filthy rivers that run by the mines? Have you smelled the air of the oil fields? Are you going to let them plunder your bodies and your souls for treasure?"

Santiago grows very red in the face. He was so pale and yellow when he first dragged into town. Our mountain air has done him good.

He gestures towards the latrines, lined up like soldiers. "A gift from the government!" he shouts. "And no one uses them. Do you know why? Of course you know why. You already know. We are humble people up here. We don't have much education. We don't have much land or many pesos. But there's one thing we know. We are not going to let the government have our shit. The government's got quite enough of its own!"

It was a wonderful fiesta and all night people talked about Santiago, that fine young man. Buy him a drink! Find him a wife!

Dominga wrapped herself in a shawl and went outside to watch our sun rise. The mists slowly lifted and the trees appeared, at times soft like velvet, sometimes harsh black, hard looking, like rocks. The trees up here are pines. Especially in the mist and when there's *chipichipi* rain you can smell not only the needles but the bark. Sometimes the earth itself, it smells like piney earth. Most of us here, we live with the natural world, but we don't think much about whether it's beautiful or not. Or we know it is. But we don't do like Dominga now, sitting outside to sigh with pleasure at the morning. Santiago might do something like that. Probably only Santiago would understand.

Once the sun was up, the air turned so clear you could have seen for miles if the peaks and cliffs weren't blocking the view, jutting out here and there. You could have seen the schools, the vegetable gardens, the new brightly painted bandstand Dominga had the men build in the plaza. You would see how the patches of cabbage stand out so distinct from the patches of squash. Everything sharp and separate and distinct. The dogs in the dust, still mangy and dirty, still covered with sores, but inoculated now, at least that. Women carrying water from the river. Boys with firewood on their backs. Smoke rising in the air and men heading off to work their parcels of land. Not the good land, but the land we've got.

And I wonder, what if instead of rising, being burnt off, what if the mists lowered again over everything, soft and gentle? What if things weren't all separate? What if we weren't put on this earth to work and to suffer?

Dominga got up and walked back into her home. Today is apparently a special day: she bathes, puts on a clean cotton dress — one of those short ones — and wears her shoes.

The inspector from the city and his driver stumbled into town about midday. They had to abandon their jeep on that bad road through the ravine. The driver slept on a bench in the municipal president's office. The inspector went from house to house with Dominga, asking questions, photographing each *lavadero* and *fogón*.

In the afternoon, he left the schoolhouse with her and she

guided him up a rocky lime-marked path. Suddenly she reached for his arm. "Look!" she whispered.

Below them, in a clearing, Santiago was putting the basketball team through some new exercise. There the boys were, leaping over piles of sacks, wriggling across the ground on their bellies, hoes held — like rifles, you would have thought — in their arms.

Dominga watched the inspector's face; he watched the healthy, rugged boys.

The conspiracy went well for a while. Santiago's people sent him shipments of books and paper. The government responded by promising Dominga five new sewing machines. Suddenly, Miahuaxtla was chosen for electrification, for a free food for infants program, for the famous pilot project to raise high-altitude sheep.

"The Mormons will be here any day now," complained Dominga's father. "We're the center of the universe now for sure."

You'll want to know about the day the sewing machines arrived. At least SEWING MACHINES is what it said on the crates — in nice big letters and even I could read it. It took two jeeps, fifteen men, and several burros to carry the load. They wore civilian clothing, those men, but my dogs know what the Army smells like. As they carried those crates into town, you would have thought all the souls in Purgatory were howling up on my ridge.

Even Dominga seemed nervous when the men told her they liked Miahuaxtla so much, they intended to stay.

Santiago left town in a hurry, on another visit to his family.

The men who returned to Miahuaxtla with him were his brothers, he said. Everyone thought his father must be some real man, to have made so many sturdy sons.

The brothers were modest and shy and didn't want the kind of welcome we usually give. They arrived at dusk, crawling low on their bellies across the open fields, carrying guns.

I see Dominga, sweet Dominga. She sits wrapped in her shawl. She squats on the ground, like we all used to do, and she rocks back and forth, remembering her mother's face mild with love, her mother pushing a steaming cob of blue corn into her hands before she left for the city the very first time. The whole idea had been to make life better.

Dominga covers her face and my eyesight fails a little, too. I can't tell you what she thought or how she looked when the first grenades exploded and the gunfire rang out. It sounded like fireworks, a great celebration, echoing over our valleys and ravines, bursting loud and clear in the mountain air.

The next day is when the earth began to hum and slide and sing. I figure people on the outside don't even know about the fighting. They think all the dead were from the earthquake. But the earthquake ended the shooting. It put an end to our small war, and to much of Miahuaxtla — what was left of it — as well.

My shack was flimsy, made of reeds. When it came down, I wasn't hurt. I watched the scene below.

I'm a man of experience. I knew the Revolution. I've known all those tremors, and four earthquakes that took many lives. But never anything like this. It buried soldiers and comrades, and Dominga's mother right along with the clothes she'd taken down to the river to wash. She never did get around to using that *lavadero* Dominga built her.

Santiago didn't survive it either. For a moment there, I thought he would, clinging to that boulder, like a lizard. I trusted his determination. I could see it, in his fingers and his spine. Below him, a new ravine opened its crazy mouth. There was nothing he could do when everything began to slide.

Did he learn anything at the end when everything started humming around him? The rising dust hid the destruction, but did he understand his *fogones* would fall just like hers? There was nothing left to shoot at. It was all finished, the cabbage buried with the squash.

There was a moment there when he must have known he was going to die. Did he see the real enemy then, when he knew he would lie battered and dead with all the others? I wondered, Did he wish in his heart he had listened to me? Did he think of Dominga? Did he regret he never held her in his arms?

Please don't ask me about Dominga, my sweet little girl. *Mi hija*. When I think of her now, that's what I call her, *m'ija*, as if she were my daughter. Dead. Tell me, if you can, why is she dead? *Mi hija*. While high on his ridge, a foolish old man escapes again with his life.

The giant country to the north is very rich. Very efficient, too. They sent their helicopters quickly. They surveyed the damage, and food and blankets rained on the earth.

Right on top of Dominga's father. Falling food or falling Mormons, it made no difference anymore. Not to him. "Here they come," he moaned, poor man. Then he was crushed.

I'm glad to say that Amalia Bautista made it through alive. We met at the site of the drop.

"It's a bomb, that's what it is," she said, but I knew better. I tore away at parachute silk to uncover the cargo. And I thought, We'll have dinner tonight.

Noodles. They sent us noodles. The alphabets spilled between my fingers, the letters that, if you learn them well enough, will turn you into a modern man. Dominga, *m'ija*, don't you think it's strange that they sent noodles?

Think of all the trouble these things brought us! I don't want to make sense of these letters. Why should I? Why should Progress happen to old Ignacio?

Old crazy, they call me, the honorary madman of San Isidro Miahuaxtla. But I can't help it if my eyes have learned to focus. I hold the golden letters in my old brown hand. C-O-M-I-D-A, they say, *food*.

What Duck?

Douglas was the only child at the holiday table, though not for long, everyone warned him. Aunt Lynn and Uncle Elliott were expecting.

"Do you plan to breast-feed?" asked Aunt Stacey.

The question took Lynn aback and made her laugh. Grandma Edie would have been surprised, too, if she'd thought about it, but she was too busy throwing glances at Doug and objecting to the topic.

Stacey said, "There's no reason to hide natural functions from children." She was annoyed to begin with because her mother had seated Jon as far from her as possible. They might be living together, but her crazy mother wouldn't put them side by side unless and until they were married.

"You haven't raised any," said Edie.

Elliott interrupted Stacey's reply. "Talking about natural, we're adopting, remember?"

Edie hadn't forgotten. She spent a lot of time thinking about the impending grandchild. Though her son hadn't mentioned anything about the baby's race or nation of origin, she had a feeling he already knew what he was getting but had decided, for the time being, not to tell.

Stacey said, "I *know*." She made more money than anyone else at the table but they all persisted in treating her like a flighty kid. "The doctors are giving hormones now."

"Hormones," echoed Lynn.

"To induce lactation," said Stacey. "So that adoptive mothers can have the experience."

"You know, you could take them, too, Elliott," Lynn suggested with a giggle, while her husband beamed at her and announced his readiness, all the while hoping it was really a joke and not another of these New Masculinity trends his generation was getting stuck with.

"If you do it, you'll pass on your immunities," said Stacey.

"And probably get cancer," Doug's mother said.

Since cancer was what her husband had died of, she was considered an expert and — though it had happened three years ago — still too fragile to contradict. Everyone shut up and Edie looked again at Doug, who started to feel bad. His sadness was shapeless and dizzying and mixed with embarrassment; he had no memories of his father at all.

Doug's mother was named Karen and she was irritated with everyone. She was having a very hard time, and being with these people wasn't helping any. The living-room floor was littered with all the expensive presents everyone had given Doug. His being fatherless was bad enough; she didn't want him spoiled as well. Karen was relieved that, at least so far, he accepted the family's prodigality without taking it for granted. At the same time, she worried that he never asked for anything and showed so little interest in his growing collection of electronic toys.

"Changing the subject . . . ," said Grandpa Leon, in a TV announcer's voice, but then he didn't say anything more. Everyone worked at eating salad.

Edie left the table for the kitchen. When Elliott, Karen, and Stacey had been growing up in this house, they fought like all children do, but she had seen to it that they always played together and shared everything. Her children had disappointed her in various ways, but what upset her most was that, aside from family dinners and holidays, they rarely saw one another. They had not grown up to be friends.

Lynn jumped up to clear the salad dishes from the table, trying to be the perfect daughter-in-law, but Edie still felt like an engineer who had lived just long enough to see all her bridges fall down.

Leon asked Stacey how work was going.

"Fine," she said. No one understood what she did, so it bored her to talk about it. Most conversations with her family bored her, and it got worse the harder they tried. Her father kept reading about computers and misusing the simplest terms, hopefully, as though he expected to blunder upon some open sesame that would make his daughter open up.

Edie brought the platter out from the kitchen and it began to make the rounds to exclamations about how good the duck looked and smelled. She returned with string beans and mashed potatoes and began to serve a portion onto Stacey's plate.

"Mother, *please*," said Stacey. "I'd rather do it *myself!*"

Edie's hand stopped in midair. She was both shocked and hurt.

Elliott howled with laughter. "Bayer aspirin, right?"

"Yeah, it must have been," said Karen. "Commercials," she explained, and Edie relaxed.

"Wait a minute," said Elliott when the platter reached him. "This is perfect. Wasn't there something with a duck? A bunch of puppies, and they say *What duck? I don't see a duck.*"

"Right," said Lynn. "It was for dog food."

"That doesn't make any sense," Karen said. "No, it was the other way round. There were all these ducklings running around sampling the dog food saying *What dog? I don't see a dog.*"

"Gravy Train," said Jon, and Leon asked Elliott to pass the butter.

"Back in the fifties," Karen told her son, "when we were children, they weren't allowed to say the word *butter* in margarine commercials."

"This is a nostalgia dinner," Elliott proclaimed, holding up and withholding the butter dish. "You'll have to ask for *the higher-priced spread.*"

"I call it butter," said Leon.

Three voices around the table chirped up, simultaneously, "*Parkay.*" This time Doug got the joke; he bounced in his chair and laughed.

Jon was feeling better about the evening. With his ex-wife, when the family began to reminisce, he had always been excluded, but this was a shared world and shared experience. He went back through his memory and came up with something, a pearl drifting through some thick shampoo, possibly Prell. None of the women was wearing pearls, though, and he couldn't figure how to work it in.

"The duck is delicious," Leon said, and everyone agreed.

They all ate in silence now, not because they had nothing

to say to one another, but because they were, at last, joined. They savored the food and concentrated, alive to everything around them. The napkin might evoke a memory, or their faces shining back from the plates, or the sparkle of the glasses in the light. Each object was capable of bringing back a classic slogan or a few bars of song. Everything was hot with meaning. The electricity completed its circuit around the table and lit them all, for a moment, with well-being and peace.

After dinner, Edie said not to bother clearing the dishes away. Everyone sat in the living room and drank coffee and tea and chatted warmly, happily, about nothing much at all until Jon put down his cup and sang, "See the U.S.A. In your Chevrolet."

"Are you suggesting it's time to hit the road?" Stacey got to her feet, but with reluctance. Outside the window, it had started to snow.

There were hugs and kisses and Jon and Stacey went out into the night. Karen noticed that Edie didn't even say anything unpleasant once they had gone. Everyone who remained began to carry the dirty dishes into the kitchen, except for Douglas, who stayed in the living room and turned on the TV. But the commercials weren't as good as when his mother was a kid, and anyway, he didn't have a brother or sister to share them with. He turned off the set and the living-room lamps and curled up on the sofa in the dark.

In the kitchen, the grown-ups were stacking things in the dishwasher and he could hear them laughing.

Then his mother's voice was more serious. "You're *not*

going to take hormones," she said, and Uncle Elliott laughed. "Where's Doug?" she asked suddenly.

"Playing with his new toys," said Grandma, and Uncle Elliott laughed again and said, "What Doug? I don't see a Doug."

The Night Life

Once, during my two weeks off, I took the bus cross-country to visit my sister in California. After riding thirty hours, I felt I was going to die. It started with a pain in my knees, like the joints had been filled in with cement and my legs cramped so bad I wondered if I'd ever walk again. There was a pain in my head and a panic, a feeling that I was someplace I shouldn't be and would never get out. A few hours later, I was too numb to notice anymore. On the trip back, when the terrible feeling hit me again, somewhere in Wyoming, I didn't pay much attention to it. I knew it would pass.

The same thing happens in the bar at around 2:30 or 3:00. That's when I watch Joey making the rounds, chatting up all the women who are still here, and I start to think I shouldn't have come. I try not to watch him when he's on the job, but there's mirrors all over the place. Whichever way I turn, I may see him with his arms around some girl.

Someone just put Joey on the spot. I can tell because he's laughing. I've noticed that when you ask him a question he can't answer, he laughs. It's not a nervous laugh, or guilty. You could describe it by reading the label off a bottle of red

wine: full-bodied, robust, and hearty. It's the kind of laugh
that makes you feel good inside, and then you forget what it
was you asked.

Joey's very good at what he does. I respect that. Since he's
been manager, *You-nique* is packed every night.

A girl comes over and asks John, my favorite bartender,
for a drink. "That Joey's a real lover," she says, and I wonder
what I'm doing here and what I'm going to do with my life,
because sitting at the bar at *You-nique* at 3:00 A.M. is like being
buried alive. Actually, it doesn't bother me much when I see
someone kiss Joey. What gets to me, though I don't let on, is
when he's standing with his arm around me and one of the
really beautiful girls looks at us and gives me the once-over,
like she's saying "Oh, baby, who are you kidding?" I'm
probably not a secure enough person to be with a guy like
Joey.

I get up to go to the ladies' room because I can feel tears on
my face and that means my makeup is getting streaked. For
a change, there's no line, but there's a woman blocking the
door. "Don't go in there," she says.

"Why not?"

"Two girls went in. And they got into the same stall.
Together."

"Hey, it's the eighties," I say. I shrug and try to move past.

"I don't care if it's the eighties. This isn't Greenwich Village," says the woman. "This is New Jersey. And I don't like
that sort of thing."

Inside the ladies' room, I look in the mirror but my
makeup is fine and I don't see any tears. Like a lot of things,
it was just a feeling, nothing actually concrete. And I know in
a while I'll be out there again and Joey will come over and

say something or give me a kiss and then it will be clear he wanted me to be here and I'm doing the right thing. The feeling will pass. It's a matter of waiting it out.

Now my face stares back at me. I feel like I'm looking down into a long long tunnel. I'm so tired. My lips are chapped from gnawing on them. Sometimes I feel like some kind of small rodent. Joey says I look like a chipmunk when I come. He says my teeth come out over my lower lip and my little hands curl up on my chest.

The two girls come out of the stall, giggling. I always say *girls* instead of *women* if they're younger than me. I'm only twenty-five, but with guys, every year counts. If you're over twenty-one, they're always worried you're putting the pressure on.

The girls were probably looking for someplace private to do a little coke. Which makes sense. It's the hour. I think just about everyone, not just me, feels it all caving in at this time of night. You get so tired, you're not even sure what you're tired of — it might even be your life. That's why I think cocaine gets to be important in the night life, if you haven't learned to wait it out.

The woman who doesn't like that sort of thing gives me a funny look when I open the door. Then I'm walking back to the bar and Joey comes up behind me and puts his arms around me, his hands on my breasts. He whispers something in my ear, but over the music, I can't catch the words, just the heat from his mouth. I back up against him and hold myself there, then I turn to face him, wondering if what he said was *I love you*, and giving him a big smile. We kiss and he puts his hand between my legs. I can't enjoy it. It embarrasses me when he does that in public, but I don't say anything because I think it's a good idea to let the other girls know exactly what the situation is between Joey and me.

"Oh, God, do you have any idea what you do to me?" he asks before he glides away.

I met Joey DeLuca five months ago, on May 18 when I drove into the city to go to a private party. Actually, my girlfriend Rosemary got the invitation as a bonus for signing up for aerobic dancing, but she never goes into Manhattan because she's allergic to the air. I work in the city, but driving I don't really know my way around. When I stopped for a light, I noticed a well-dressed black man standing on the corner, so I rolled down the window and asked directions.

He said he was headed that way himself and if I gave him a lift, he'd show me, so I let him in the front seat. Before I knew what was happening, he opened the back door and three more guys piled in. *Uh oh,* I thought. *I've had it.*

They were all high. They told me they were lawyers and were going to a party at the senior partner's house. When the guy in the front seat mentioned the name of the firm, I recognized it, a big Wall Street firm. They said, *Why don't you come with us?* and I figured I'd really lucked out.

The young "lawyers" turned out to work in the mail room. We hadn't even been served drinks when a gentleman came over to escort us out. "We'll discuss your separation from the firm tomorrow," he said.

We couldn't separate ourselves from the party right away because two men were blocking the door. The older one with silver hair drew his mouth back to smile and said, "Thank you, Joseph. Thank you so much." And that was where I first saw Joey.

I don't know how to describe him really, because there's more to Joey than meets the eye. He stands very straight. He has good posture. You notice that about him, but you also notice right away he has a loose easy way of moving. There's a slight intellectual-looking indentation on the side of his nose, the kind you get from wearing glasses. Actually, it's from where a cat scratched his face when he was a little boy. His best feature? I like Joey's eyes a lot. They're very dark and slightly arched, like a deer or some kind of animal more than a man. I shiver sometimes to think how close that cat came with its claws. But what I really love is his skin. It's very smooth and very warm. Joey always carries a disposable razor and little packets of lotion and shaving cream. During the night at *You-nique,* he'll go into the back room and shave once or maybe twice, so that his cheeks are always perfectly smooth. Then he pats on some lotion. When he walks around the bar, all the girls want to kiss him on the lips. Obviously, I do, too, but I love to kiss his cheeks. And sometimes, in the middle of the night, it feels so good to touch his face with my hand. Maybe it's late and I feel drained, then I just touch Joey's face and I feel how soft it is and I feel the hot flush inside and I know this is life, real life.

The silver-haired lawyer said, "Why don't you stay awhile? Join us?"

Joey had never laid eyes on me before, but he pointed at me and said, "I've got a date."

"Oh, both of you, of course. I didn't realize she was with you."

The mail-room guys looked at each other like *What did you expect?* and the door closed behind them and Joey led me

into the living room. A man in a tuxedo came by with a tray
and Joey took a glass of white wine for each of us.

"You better tell me your name," he said.

I felt funny, not about him, but about the party. I was
wearing a hot pink polka dot skirt, real short, that stood out
like an old-fashioned crinoline, a wide, shiny black belt, and
a black fake-leather-look shirt tucked in. My gold metallic
bag was across my chest like a bandit's cartridge belt and I
had spiked my hair. No one else in the room looked anything
like me. Some of the older women wore sequins and beads,
but all the others, closer to my age, were real subdued,
pigeon-colored. You could tell their clothes cost money,
though. I figured same as the phone book — you pay more
not to be listed. People were too polite to stare, but that didn't
make me feel any better.

"I don't like being used," said Joey, very close to my ear. "I
come to this party. I thought I was invited. I mean, as *myself*.
Then I see they're just counting on me to bring the coke."

"*These* people . . . ?"

"Yeah," he said. "Surprised? It's the old ones," he added.
"The big shots. What do they have to lose?"

I said, "Wow." I felt very naïve.

"Let's get out of here," he said. "I know a place that's real
relaxed. If you don't mind going to Jersey. Anyway, you'll
like my friends."

"I don't know," I said. I didn't tell him, not right then,
that I was from Jersey, too. I wondered how much he was
into drugs. I'm a very cautious person and it got me a little
nervous that he was the type who would be counted on to
bring the coke. I also wondered what was going on at the
party Rosemary had been invited to, if I might meet some

interesting people there. Sometimes at parties I get so bored.

"Come on," said Joey. "Take a few risks."

He brought me here, to *You-nique*. He didn't want to dance at first, and I said, "Not dance at a disco?" Finally we went out under the flashing lights. After we'd danced for a while, we left the floor with our arms around each other. That's when we really touched for the first time.

"I'm so glad I met you tonight," Joey said and we kissed and I moved closer into his arms. Then I felt it. It was an electric shock, the way I reacted. In biology once, we did something that made frogs jerk that way. First we put a needle through their brains. Joey has jolts sometimes in his sleep and he cries out. Once I said, "It's all right," and I tried to hold him. "Doesn't that ever happen to you?" he asked. He was annoyed at me for making a big deal over nothing. "It's called a clonic jerk," he said. "Everyone gets them."

I get them sometimes. When it's strong enough, it wakes me and I feel like I'm falling and the room is spinning. I feel I might throw up. I know it doesn't mean anything, but still, I would like to have someone hold me and say it's OK, until it passes. But I know it will pass anyway.

"You have a gun," I said.

"Yeah. Protection. There's a contract out on me." Then he squeezed me. "That's a joke," he said. "Actually, it's not even loaded, tonight. I'm just getting used to carrying it. I start work here Tuesday night. Manager. And *this*" — he tapped the bulge under his arm — "this is part of the job." He held up his hand like taking an oath. "Licensed and everything." He pulled my head to his chest. "I'm sorry if it took you by surprise. I should have warned you. You were bound to find out sooner or later."

Later, when I went home with him, I watched him take off the shoulder holster. "Look," he said. "I'll show you it's not loaded."

"No. Please put it away."

"I really like you," he said. "It's weird. You're so straight. I don't usually feel so comfortable, so good, I mean real good, with someone like you. I think I need you."

Joey comes around the bar and kisses me on the forehead. He's wearing a new jacket. "Hey, look at the back for me, will you?" He's paranoid about getting a cigarette burn. The jacket feels soft. I think maybe it's cashmere but I'm afraid to ask.

"You got some change?" he asks. "I got to make a call."

Joey seems keyed up tonight and I think something's wrong. He could get change behind the bar. I find some coins in my purse and lay them on his palm. I think it's not money he needs, but a token, some proof that someone's with him, that he still has the magic touch of getting what he needs.

Then he's gone. I worry about him, what it's going to do to him, living the night life. Still, it could be worse.

Before I met him, Joey used to be a driver for the Family. At first, I thought he meant *his* family. Then I understood. He must have been a bodyguard, too, because I think that's part of what a Mob driver has to do. When he told me about it, I was pretty upset, but when he explained it to me, I could understand. He's not proud of it. He feels very very guilty about that part of his life, in spite of the fact that he never hurt anyone — Joey's basically a gentle person. He's just glad now that it's all in the past.

The thing is, Joey's mother never expected him to accomplish anything, to be anyone. She encouraged him to think small, so he had no serious thought-out goals. That's why he says he understands women so well, because in some ways, we were brought up the same, with the same handicap: nothing expected of us but family obligations.

It's true my mother didn't encourage me to set high goals either. The difference is, Joey's mother didn't think he could hack it and my mother didn't think I'd ever need it. So I did the ordinary — learned to type and stayed at my first job for almost four years. When I decided to leave home and move out on my own, my mother was upset, but she didn't stop me. She did say, "Don't buy anything." I furnished the apartment with the junk people were giving away or leaving out on the street. "This is just temporary," my mother said. "You'll get all that stuff new when you get married." I love cats, but my mother said, "Don't get one. Your husband might be allergic." That's how she talks, as though my husband has been picked out, ordered, and paid for, and we're waiting for Macy's to deliver.

The first time Joey saw my place, he said, "This won't do. Is this what you think of yourself?" If I ever really pull myself up, a lot of the credit will belong to Joey. He's always saying, "Don't down yourself," and getting me to look at myself differently.

My mother has started to see some things differently these days. Suddenly she's into careers. "I never had the chance," she tells me. "Now all the young women are doctors and lawyers. Why don't you make something of yourself?"

The fact is, I'd like a more challenging job. Sometimes, the only word I can give you for my job is *deadening*. I think I could be an administrative assistant, someone's right arm. I'm organized and pay attention to detail. As it is, I balance my boss's checkbooks and handle my own correspondence. Last year, he asked me to do his income tax, but I refused. "What's the matter?" he asked. "Math anxiety?" I just didn't want to know how much he makes and I told him so.

Sometimes, behind the typewriter, I think of Joey. My fingers keep moving automatically, but inside I shiver and ache. It's wonderful to want someone that bad. Then I realize for years I might as well have been sleepwalking. My life was nothing for a long long time.

I haven't told my mother anything about Joey because I like to talk about him and so I know I'd end up saying too much. Then she'd tell me I'm being a fool. I know he has his faults. Drugs, for example. He's got a real problem, there. But he'll beat it. It'll pass and I don't want to say anything now that people will hold against him later.

I watch what I say to people, because when you get into anything with them, I find that I hear a lot of bullshit. Most of what people know is what they hear on TV, and a lot of it isn't true. Like about the Mob. Joey says there's connected and then there's *connected*, and it's not at all the same. But most people have this simplistic view. The first thing they'll tell you is that once you're in, you're in for life. I used to believe that, but now I know different. When Joey said he wanted out, he wanted to quit and go to college, there were no hard feelings. Everyone could see a guy like Joey was looking for something else. Everybody wished him well and he quit and he went and that was that.

Joey says you need — people need — meaning in life. You wouldn't guess looking at him that he thinks about things like that, but Joey's seen a lot. He knows this rich guy, who's a philanthropist. This guy made a ton of money, but it didn't mean enough. He wanted to do something positive, to help others, so he opened up youth centers in the worst parts of Newark, recreation halls where teenagers could get off the streets and hang out. The guy has millions, but Joey says he's real down-to-earth. He says when I meet him, I'll love him. Anyway, the guy gave Joey a part-time job to help him through college. Joey says he liked it. He handled himself fine with all those tough ghetto kids and he was able to recommend some of them to the rich guy for jobs. When Joey graduated, he started going for his MBA, but he didn't like it much and quit. I think the problem is that he still doesn't have faith in himself, but anyway, the rich guy owns *Younique* and he made Joey manager.

I can see the job is an opportunity, but I don't see how it solves Joey's thing about meaning in life. Now I watch him. It's frightening to know someone so well that you can tell when something's wrong. Joey's talking to a lot of *men* tonight, and I've noticed that usually when he spends time with men, money changes hands. But not tonight.

I always notice about the money. It's not that I'm greedy, but it's hard to have plans without cash. Or rather, you can have plans, but you can't make them happen. I dream of having my own catering business someday or a restaurant. I love to cook, though these days, I don't even eat regular meals let alone cook them. All I need is the capital to get started. I don't see how I can do it without. My mother says I should find a rich husband. In the meantime, they're training me on the word processor, so I won't quit my job. I've been thinking lately there are law firms that have people working nights. They pay good for the late shift and depending how things go between Joey and me, it might be the right move. It makes it hard now, my having a day job. I get home from the office, take a nap if I can. Then I drive over here and wait for Joey to get off and close up. Then we go for breakfast. If he's not too tired, we go back to his place and then, when he's sleeping, I get dressed and head back to work.

If I worked nights, most of those firms will pay to send you home in a taxicab and I could get dropped off right here. Joey knows all those Wall Street lawyers and he could probably help me get a job. The only trouble is, I'd be getting kind of dependent on Joey. If I get here by cab, it would make him responsible for getting me home. That might be pushing it. I have to wait and see.

So far I've figured it pretty good. The first night we spent together, Joey didn't ask for my number or anything, but he kept reminding me he was going to be working here on Tuesday. He repeated it one or two times. I wasn't sure if I was reading him right, but that Tuesday night, you can guess where I was.

Now everybody knows me, but it was different the first time I walked into *You-nique* alone. There I was, in a place that serves the public, wondering if I had the right to be there. My stomach was so knotted up, that's why I had to order ginger ale. I was afraid I was throwing myself at Joey, making a pest of myself, cramping his style.

He hurried over as soon as he saw me. "You came!" he said. He gave me a big kiss in front of everybody and told the bartender, "Be sure this lady has whatever she wants." I wondered if he remembered my name, so I introduced my-self to the bartender, very distinctly.

"I'm sorry I can't stay here with you," Joey said.

"That's all right," I said. "You're on the job. I understand."

He smiled and kissed me again and said, "I'm glad you're here. Did I say that already? I'm really glad," and I knew I'd done the right thing.

This girl comes over and asks for a kamikaze. John pulls the bottles and mixes the drink. That's more challenging to him than tapping me a ginger ale. I drink it in a beer mug. Close up, it doesn't fool anyone because it doesn't have a head, but at least when Joey goes by fast and sees me with a mug in my hand, he doesn't stop and say, "Come on. Live a little."

Before I met Joey, I was a very boring person.

"You're Joey's friend," says the girl. She giggles. She's real young, but she has circles under her eyes like I do, hidden with Erace. But then how do you hide the Erace? It looks too pale on her. Terrible, in fact. I wonder if it looks that bad on me. I recognize her. She said something earlier.

Now she says, "I go with Richie." Richie's the new DJ, a friend of Joey's. "I wanted to talk to you because of what I said before," she says. "About Joey being a lover. I mean, I wouldn't know. I go with Richie. All I meant was Joey's real smooth, and the way everyone here likes him."

She has more energy than I do. She has a fast, eager way of talking.

"That's OK," I say.

She says, "I know what it's like. That's why I wouldn't do anything to hurt you. I know Richie goes home sometimes with other women. What can I do? It's an occupational hazard, and anyway, he's not ready for a commitment."

I smile at her. What else can I do?

"The only mistake I made with him, and it was a big one," she says . . .

". . . was falling in love.

"Yeah." She closes her eyes. "It wasn't *his* fault."

"No," I say. "He didn't tell you to."

"Told me *not* to." She giggles. "He's never lied to me. That means more to me than anything."

"Yeah. Joey's like that," I say. "He wouldn't tell a lie."

"And he's good to me. And you know what really gets me? Is how he handles himself. In a sticky situation, like with other women and everything, he keeps it from getting messy. He never hurts anyone's feelings. He handles it so well."

"I really admire that in a man," I say. I always thought it was Joey's you-nique skill. Maybe it's just a hustle all night-life people learn. But that isn't fair. Richie and Joey are buddies. It makes sense for buddies to have the same style.

Joey must see the other women in the afternoon. I mean, he leaves here with me every night. I wish I could lie down with him sometimes at 5:00 P.M. instead of A.M., when for a change I'd feel fresh and strong, when I could look at him and gaze at him, without fighting to keep my eyes open.

Richie's girl says, "What he loves most about me is my patience. But sometimes I don't know that I'm doing him a favor. Sometimes I wonder what would happen if I said, *I can't take this anymore*."

I think I know: he'd shake his head and say, *Then you're not my kind of girl*, like he's more sorry for her than for himself.

I'm always afraid that one of these days Joey is going to say to me, *You know, this isn't working.*

"The thing is," says Richie's girl, "I care. Maybe I shouldn't, but I care very deeply."

I look at her. She's young, real young. She asks for another kamikaze and downs it in a single gulp.

"You have a day job?" I ask.

"Yeah," she says. "It makes it hard."

"I know. But don't give up your day job. No matter what else you lose, you've got something when you work days."

She nods. "I know. It's the life. What this life does to people. Richie, I think Richie is really a fine person. He needs something steady to hold on to."

I think of Joey saying to me, "You're so good for me. Oh, God, you're so good."

Richie's girl is waiting for me to agree with her. I say, "You ever think sometimes that you're fooling yourself?"

She grips her empty shot glass and doesn't answer.

"Have you noticed?" I say. "Only women hang out here. Men, they have to get their beauty sleep so they can go to the office every morning and get ahead in the world. Did you notice? The only men here this late — look around — just the guys who work here. You know what their job is? Tickling our insides and taking our cash."

"Richie puts my drinks on his tab," she says.

"I was talking about women," I tell her, "in general. I wasn't talking about you and me."

"Excuse me," she says. "I have to go to the ladies'."

These nights go on forever. You've got to understand, I sit through eight hours at my own job. Then I've got to sit through another eight hours at his. It's not like the office, there's no clock on the wall and I don't like people to see me always checking my watch. If Joey thinks I'm not having a good time, he might tell me to stay home. Sitting here, I end up with too much time to think and I wonder if I'm being mistreated and if this is any way to live and where is the meaning in my life. Sometimes I ask another woman to dance. Mostly to kill time, but also for the exercise. But they mostly don't want to.

When Joey comes over and kisses me and says, "Tired, aren't you?" in a gentle voice, I don't have to look at my watch to know it's closing time.

"Ummm." I put my head against him. Then I feel him get stiff in his arms and chest and he holds me apart from him for a moment.

"Don't go anywhere," he says. "I got to talk to my cousin."

He's gone, but I see him in the mirror. Joey's at the table near the door. This guy's standing there with his collar turned up and they talk for a while. It looks like Joey's on the spot, but he doesn't use his laugh. His cousin slaps him on the shoulder before he leaves and I get the feeling that Joey's in some kind of trouble.

I understand Joey. That doesn't mean I can predict what he'll do and it doesn't mean that I know all the details. There are lots of things we don't talk about, but still, I can tell when he's scared.

I've learned from Joey that you don't have to talk about everything when you're close to someone. If there's anything I have to know, he'll tell me. If he's in trouble, all he really wants from me, I think, is a gesture, to let him know I'm on his side, standing by. You can be there for someone without words. I don't want to see Joey get hurt.

When he comes back to me, his smile is just a twitch. "You about ready for breakfast?" he asks.

"Yeah," I say. "I'm famished."

There are things I want that I don't have, mostly things that money can't buy. But basically, as far as survival goes, I can take care of myself. I'm not like Joey. I don't take a lot of risks. I have nothing to be afraid of.

Sometimes I feel sorry for Joey. I put my hand against his face. I can feel a pulse tremble, in my fingers or maybe inside his cheek.

"How about pancakes?" I say.

He says, "Great," and I take his arm and say, "Joey, today it's on me."

Wonderful Baby

Kerisha danced around the room and her T-shirt popped up from her pants and out popped a belly button, out popped a band of brown around her little body, out popped a strip of color, skin. Everything else in the room was gray, her aunt, the baby, even the pink stripes on Kerisha's running shoes. It was gray because of the air, because of the plastic on the windows, because of the month of the year and the burning. The air in the room was only half-air, dirty air, gray air. Kerisha didn't care. She stretched the way a cat would stretch if a cat was a little girl. She ran her hands along her legs and stroked her own arms and rubbed inside her shirt. Oh she was soft soft and smooth. Oh she was warm warm and young. Kerisha danced because she was playing and she was playing because she would soon be eight. Eight eight eight. Too late. Old. Worse things happen then. Kerisha shook her body. She rotated her hands in the gray air.

"In and out," she sang. "Take my cherry. In and out."

Her aunt knew the song. She mouthed the words and bounced the rhythm with her bottom on the couch. She moved the baby's arms like pistons, first one, then the other, back and forth.

Kerisha danced near her aunt. She wanted to look at the baby but she didn't want to. The baby might make her think of her brother, her sister, her other little sister, her mother. "In and out, in and out." She bumped into her aunt, who aimed a swat.

The baby might make her think of home.

"I'll change him," sang Kerisha. "I know how."

Look at me! she thought. Look at me! Her little nipples were flat, and gleeful as jingle bells.

Her aunt didn't look. "I didn't get to be this age not knowing."

Kerisha stood still a moment and now the room danced. It spun around and twirled and shook. The gray air spun and turned to wind, it blew around her ears and under her clothes, the air was greasy and dry like sticky ash. She skipped rope without a rope: Seven bad. Eight worse. Her aunt age worse worse. Kerisha stood on tiptoes, testing it, being big. When the baby got bigger, when it had more hair, she would comb it. She had combed her brother's, his head on her lap, in her hand the pick, and she'd touched the pick to his neck, lightly, then a little harder, then harder, to see if it tickled or hurt. "I want to go home," she said.

"Can't," said her aunt.

Kerisha started dancing again.

She knows all forward movement is decline. Today the apartment is shabby and cold. Move down the street to tomorrow, where there's holes in the ceilings and walls, where filthy water from the toilet upstairs drips into your room and on your bed and on your table and on your head

as you climb the stairs, and next week the building's con-
demned and you live behind the placard, the *black card*,
everyone says, and you're not supposed to be there, and
then there's no more filth leaking because the water's off,
and you can't see the filth because there's no light and next
month is coming when the building will be an empty shell.
This is natural law. If the room were to shoot up on stilts, if
the room grew one hundred feet tall, if the room turned into
an observation tower, this is what you would see: a splash of
fresh paint on a wall is a revolutionary act.

Kerisha danced and the girlfriends showed up, the friends
of her aunt, giggling and whispering and whooping, stomp-
ing in the door. One pulls the other close to whisper in her
ear, the other shoves her away and laughs. They touch and
push, they whisper and tell each other off, and this is a
pleasure. The room tingled with pleasure, though her aunt
sat on the sofa and hardly looked up to say hello.

When the girlfriends are together, there's a feeling of
severed flesh, like one wounded thing, pressing itself
against itself to shield the part that's raw and quick. The
girls sat around on the couch staring at the baby. There's a
promise of wholeness. If they draw close enough, long
enough, flesh will knit to flesh, the scar will seal them like a
zipper, sew them together like a seam, they will be one.
One of them bent over the baby as if to coo, and blew her
cigarette smoke into its face. The baby shook its head. The
girls lean in, then pull apart, they lean in, then pull apart. If
they are close enough, the scar will bond, and then when
they separate, they will rend and tear, they will rip and
strip to the bone.

One of the girlfriends was laughing. Her shoulders shook

and it could have been sobs but no, it was laughter, because her eyes smiled and glittered and the sides of her mouth both turned up and tightened. She was laughing and holding it in. Mmmmm, she puckered her lips and bent over the baby. She pressed the red end of her cigarette into the baby's foot. The baby screamed.

The baby's mother pulled back but her friend was smiling. The girls all sat around the baby, closing in and watching, and their friend, the oldest, most inventive one of all, pressed the cigarette into the baby's other foot. The baby screamed.

This time, the girls screamed too with delight. The baby had screamed. It screamed once and then it screamed again. The mother took the cigarette and touched it to the dimple of the baby's knee. The baby screamed. The mother sat back, startled, and smiled at her friends. She passed the cigarette on. Now the baby was burned on its hand. It screamed. It still worked. The girls exchanged glances, shook their heads, wondering. The baby was burned on its stomach. It screamed.

The baby did the same thing each time, and in between, it made the same wailing sounds. You knew exactly what it would do. You did one thing, the baby did the other. You knew in advance exactly what it would do. But would it do it again? It did. The mother was happy. Her baby made her proud. She lived in a good place, she had a healthy baby, she wasn't like some she could name. She leaned over and showered the little body with kisses. She burned the other knee. The baby screamed.

Kerisha was dancing. "Look at me!" sang Kerisha. "Look at me!"

Now there were three cigarettes, one for each girl. They were intent and happy, feeling something they'd known once and could only vaguely recall. They were interested. Curious, learning, they loved the logical beauty of it. They loved law, the predictable, controllable nature of the observed phenomenon. They laughed.

The baby had been born light brown and grew darker every day. The scars would heal even darker brown, smooth round chocolate knobs. In some places, the cigarettes had burned deeper, down to where blood was red, flesh pink.

The girls wanted the feeling to go on. Unlike any other feeling they knew, they could make it go on. They made it happen, they brought it from the inside, observing worlds, unlocking doors.

Kerisha was dancing. She wondered what was going on over there on the couch, but she couldn't stop. She danced as if the dance was dancing her, as if someone was moving her arms and legs, her bottom and her hips, as if some big hands were making her squirm, tickling, as if she wanted to do one thing but some big man was making her do another, as if yes, she wanted to do the one thing, yes, now now, look at me, more! She danced as if there were ten and eleven and a hundred and a thousand cute little things swarming on her, she tried to shake them off, she tried to shake off the hands and the man's mouth and all the rest, she gritted her teeth to grind him, she shook her arms and her hips and the skin on her body crawled and she shook herself as if she were a dog and her shoulders shrugged up to wiggle free and she danced as if she were pressed up against a wall, against a floor, or on a bed, with butterflies in her stomach, choking, out of breath, crying, excited, in pain, dancing, as if she were on a stage, in the spotlight, doing a TV commercial for millions and millions of dollars and everyone was watching and her mother sat there applauding with that man by her side. "In and out," she sang. "Cherry cherry cherry cherry cherry."

The girls laughed and the baby screamed. Kerisha danced to the couch and nosed in among the girlfriends like a dog. The baby lay on the couch and Kerisha slipped her hand fast inside the diaper. Yes, a boy. And someone said, "The Devil in you," and hit her so hard, she thought of her mother. She fell to the floor, she couldn't hear a thing. Maaaa, she thought. I want to go home.

"Can't," said her aunt.

Kerisha lay on the floor. Yes yes again. Her hands, palms down by her shoulders, she pushed. Up she went backwards into a back bend, warm and supple as a cat. Her body hummed. Someone at the door. Like a cat she sprang, *up!* The man?

It was a girl with a camera, a nice camera. Where did she get it? Who knows? Everyone posed. The girlfriends grouped together and Kerisha's aunt held the baby, her hands under its arms, she held it up. "Closer," said the girl with the camera. Closer, closer, and the open wounds for a moment brushed and touched and Kerisha ran over and joined the picture there at the side, hand on cocked hip, elbow angling out, her hand waving to secret admirers, her smile.

The girlfriends jumped apart and the camera spat out paper like a receipt. The picture appeared before their eyes. Everyone laughed and passed the picture from hand to hand until the blurry faces came clear and then someone dropped the photo on the floor. The girls went back to their game and showed their friend, and she took pictures till there wasn't any film.

When the baby stopped screaming, the girls went on laughing until they noticed that something was different, something was wrong. Something was lost. They tried to remember what it had been, what things had been like only moments before. They tried to figure out what was gone. They concentrated, and suddenly concentration pulled them like a vacuum like a rewinding tape on high speed like a fall down an elevator shaft in the highest rise of projects through the silence and the deadness to a time so far back it might be before memory, because the girls didn't remember the time, they just felt it, the memory of a promise given by no one they could remember. *When you hurt me, I cry out, when you hurt me, I cry out,* something like that, simple and easy to follow; something that implied an *I* and a *me*; something clear like light, not gray air; and warmth, not fire; and as easy to see through as a window that has not been sealed up with plastic or cinder block or brick.

The girls were silent. The baby was silent. It lay, not moving now, on the couch and the girls looked at it and at the marks on its body and remembered that a moment ago it had cried out and moved.

"Jesus save me!" cried one of the girls.

The mother snatched up her baby and held it to her. "My baby!" she screamed, remembering. "Oh, my child!"

The room rose straight up in the air, higher and higher with the enormity of it all, and so high that the girlfriends knew they were looking down and knew they were tiny and unseen, and from those heights you couldn't see beyond but only down, and you could see glowing scars on the earth, fires where people kept warm and fires where abandoned buildings were consumed, where the buildings were called *abandoned* but the firemen had to go in anyway because people lived there. *People,* they said, *and I use the term loosely,* and the gray wind ripped through the room.

"No," howled the girlfriends. "Noooooooo . . ."

The baby cried. The mother put it on the floor on its back and it squirmed and she forgot it. The girls sat on the couch and laughed.

Kerisha was dancing, but she no longer wanted anyone to see her. Her eyes were closed, her feet a hard fast danger to the baby on the floor. Now her dancing wasn't movement. It was a posture, then a pose. Now her dancing moved inside, as though her body had moved inside her head, as though you could touch her and she wouldn't know it. Next her head would move inside her head, but not yet. She was dancing for herself and she was dancing for the wonderful baby. See, this is how. She would take care of him. Yes. Even the unfulfilled intention is visionary here. Kerisha was rigid but the secret hips were still shaking and the tiny shoulders and the arms and legs shrinking down in size, and the feelings were still shaking though she wasn't sure anymore they were hers. See, this is how. In and out.

Huggers

How do you protect your child against a dangerous world without telling her ugly things she shouldn't have to know? Joanne had finally laid down a single, inflexible rule: No one touches you but your mother. So when Rhonda let them into Liz's apartment, the women hugged and Joanne fingered Rhonda's new earrings, but six-year-old Samantha slipped discreetly past, the way she had been taught to do. Then Joanne hurried to the bed and threw her arms around Liz.

"How *are* you?" she asked.

Liz, in her burgundy-colored silk robe, sat at the edge of the bed, quilt and pillows in disarray, cigarette in one hand, phone trapped between shoulder and ear. Allison massaged the back of her neck. The fragrance of roses was overwhelming, from the flowers by the bed and from the Tea Rose perfume that Liz had copied from Rhonda and Allison had copied from Liz.

Allison had brought the flowers. Ordinarily Liz picked up a bunch every morning after her run, but last night's trouble had left her too upset to go out.

"Joanne is here," Liz said into the phone as she hugged

back. She often cited studies that showed that people who were hugged every day lived longer. The friends dispensed this therapeutic benefit freely to one another, like mothers measuring out daily doses of some surprisingly delicious cod-liver oil.

"We have to mother each other and lover each other," Liz liked to say. Women like them couldn't expect understanding from their own mothers, the world had changed too much. And men, good for some things, were generally inadequate.

Joanne had been intimidated by Liz at one time. Then, hugging her had been an act of courage and, because Liz welcomed it, Joanne gained confidence each time she did it, until whenever they were together now, she could hardly restrain herself from touching Liz. Things had changed, though, since Samantha was born. Being entirely responsible for someone else took you out of yourself. It made you grow up. Liz, for all her strength, still needed people. So many people. Did she really have to get everyone up so early on a Saturday morning? Joanne had hurried over, thinking Liz was all alone.

"My turn," said Allison, opening her arms.

Samantha pulled Liz's cat out from under the bed, held it tight, and watched while the grown-ups clutched each other.

"Oh, God, not *that* coffeepot!" Liz shouted across the room to Rhonda in the kitchen alcove. "I'm in imminent danger of having my pearls melted," she said into the phone. "That's where I hide the good stuff," she explained. "That's the only reason they didn't make off with it. . . ."

There had only been one man, actually, but a *he* who made

off with your pearls would sound no worse than a nasty boyfriend.

"I was coming back from Kansas City, and you'd think after what I tipped the cabbie he would have waited to see I got inside . . ." *They* had pushed into the building behind her. "No, I wasn't hurt, but I feel *violated. Violated,*" she repeated, still so shaken, she thought this was an original idea.

Katharine sat in the corner reading a magazine, like a private-duty nurse during the family's visit. Joanne went to embrace her. Hugging Liz made her feel strong; hugging Katharine gave her a thrill of pride: Joanne loved the fact that their crowd was integrated now. She remembered to say *Katharine,* not *Kathy;* nicknames and diminutives were demeaning and no longer in use, except for Liz, who broke all the rules.

Liz could get away with it because she ran her own computer graphics business and didn't have to act professional in front of a boss. She had recently made Katharine her vice president. "I don't know what the problem is," she liked to say to other businesspeople who complained about affirmative action. "*I* had no trouble finding a qualified black woman." After the mugging, it was Katharine she had called first. *They* had taken Liz's keys, and until the locksmith came to change the locks, she was afraid to be alone.

Katharine had stayed the night, though she was allergic to cigarette smoke, while Liz talked to all her friends on the West Coast, where it was still a reasonable enough hour to call. Now Katharine yawned and closed her eyes. Only a headache kept her from dozing off. She had heard the story a couple of dozen times.

"Who wants decaf and who wants the real thing?" Rhonda called. She waved a hand to get attention and set her clunky bracelets jangling; she no longer sat behind a typewriter all day and liked to wear impractical jewelry to prove it.

"Of course I screamed," said Liz into the phone. "But it's summer. People are away. Anyway, with all the windows closed and the air conditioners humming, who could hear?"

The air conditioner in Liz's apartment was on high, dripping a puddle on the rug, but with so many people in the room, the air had taken on a sluggish warmth, reminiscent of the office.

Liz hung up and dialed again. "Oh, Margaret!" she said, bursting into tears. "You'll never imagine what's happened." Liz had a theory that words could both intensify and alienate emotion. The first time you put a tentative feeling into words, you gave birth to it. But as you repeated it, the experience itself would recede, become a story, an object, until you could remove it from your affective life and look at it with detachment. If she told the story of her mugging often enough, if she let it harden into a script, she would eventually overcome the outrage and fear.

Monica had a key and let herself in. She had been hired a year ago to clean Liz's apartment once a week, but as Liz explained, "My employees always become my friends." Her arrival set off another round of hugs and kisses. She looked around, smiling. "Well, we're all here."

"Where's Birgit?" Joanne asked, annoyed that someone from their crowd had managed not to come. Birgit was probably at the beach. And Tamara. She was missing, too.

Monica helped Rhonda serve the coffee, along with the Danish she'd brought, guessing that there would be a full house and a refrigerator with nothing in it but coffee and vitamin pills. Joanne took one pastry for herself and one to hand to her daughter; she avoided letting anyone else give Samantha treats.

Tamara appeared with more flowers — a surprise; she was known to be cheap. Allison and Joanne discovered they had both planned to visit Sarah later in the day. Liz was giving someone career advice over the phone.

"Coffee?" offered Rhonda, something she had never done when she was still Tamara's secretary. It was Liz who had convinced her to quit and go back to school, much to Tamara's relief. She had found Rhonda useless and stupid but hadn't known how to fire her.

"How's school?" she asked.

Rhonda didn't like her former boss, but she appreciated her being so supportive; a man would have wanted to keep her in her place. She began to tell about the summer session, but Tamara had turned to Joanne without waiting for a reply.

Rhonda stood a moment, lost, with no one to pour coffee for. People could understand that Liz might take on someone like Rhonda to improve her, but what was inexplicable was that Liz actually copied things from Rhonda, such as the Tea Rose perfume, which was entirely out of character; Liz was not sweet.

"Know what you need?" Rhonda asked. "A manicure. You need to feel taken care of . . ."

Behind her magazine, Katharine shook her head and furrowed her brow.

"Well, I can't go get a manicure," said Liz at last, after making everyone wait a moment to see how she was going to respond. "I can't go anywhere until the locksmith comes. And besides, I've got guests."

"She makes house calls," Rhonda said. "At a time like this, you need to be pampered."

If you paid for a manicure, thought Joanne, who was doing the pampering? The manicurist, or Liz herself, who would supply the cash? And if you pampered *yourself*, didn't that defeat the whole point, which was to get someone to take care of you? Anyway, she thought, *children* should be pampered, not adults.

"Oh, what's the use?" Liz asked. "Look at these hands. I don't even have any nails."

"She'll give you artificial," said Rhonda.

Liz tapped a finger against the phone. "Will she take a check? A personal check?"

"Well, she knows me," Rhonda said.

"Then let's get her over here. She can do everyone." Samantha lifted her face from the cat's fur a moment, listening and wondering if she would be included. "It's on me," said Liz. "We'll make a party out of this."

This, too, was the way Liz did things. She believed single women are by nature depressed, that every depressive has the right to an occasional manic phase, and that by turning the tables on circumstance, you could swing into that manic phase and stick there.

It was settled. Rhonda circulated, advising everyone on what color to choose. She was the expert who read women's magazines the way the others read their professional journals. Tamara couldn't stand her. The first day Rhonda had come to work, she'd sharpened all her pencils and then left the office, returning hours later with a toy koala bear that she placed soberly and precisely at the back right-hand corner of her desk, as though this was a skill she'd learned at some exclusive secretarial school.

"What would we do without each other?" sighed Liz with contentment. She had put aside the phone and stubbed out the last cigarette. Waiting for the manicurist, drinking their coffee, the women looked around at one another and marveled at the community they had built. Rhonda had accompanied Allison when she needed her abortion. Tamara had picked up Samantha from school when she was sick and Joanne was arguing a case in court and couldn't get away. Allison, who usually woke early, walked Tamara's dogs. They sent each other flowers for their birthdays, cheered each other up when their men did them wrong, made each other herbal teas for menstrual cramps.

Women do so much for their friends, thought Tamara. She imagined how much more they gave their lovers. She sometimes considered becoming a lesbian and liked to think about the sort of woman who would be her type. Tamara loved most of the women in the room, but not one of them was quite right. Since she wasn't attracted to female bodies, she would want someone small, with not a lot of body to deal with. If she were going to turn, it would have to be for someone special: a woman who was petite and adorable and who had money. Someone along the lines of Linda Ronstadt.

"We are a society of our own," said Liz. "Completely interdependent."

"That's what makes this so *political*," said Birgit, who had just been let in the door. Her most recent political act had been to crop off her long platinum hair. Now she wore a buzz cut, hennaed a particularly artificial red.

"I'd better be getting over to Sarah's," said Joanne.

"But what about your nails?"

"And," Birgit objected, "I've brought champagne."

"Champagne!" shouted Liz, delighted. "At a time like this, champagne!" To Liz, having fun during a crisis was good therapy; to Birgit, it was an organizing tool.

Monica got the good glasses; she knew where everything was kept. Birgit popped the cork and poured.

"This reminds me of the last time we all drank champagne together," Liz said. "Remember? That time you all helped me dig out from under?" Though it was hard to imagine Liz falling apart, she did now and then, on purpose, some people said, to make herself more approachable. The last time was after a bad love affair. For months, newspapers, magazines, and take-out food containers accumulated on the floor, and dishes piled up in the sink.

Finally, Birgit had called all the friends. "Liz would feel a lot better," she said, "if her place weren't such a mess. But it's so bad at this point, and she's so down, there's no way she can handle it alone." Besides, housework was drudgery for one person, but as a group effort, it could be fun. Back in the sixties, Birgit had spent a weekend in the slums as part of a community cleanup campaign. "We all went down with mops and disinfectant and paint. People there had given up hope, but we showed them what a little effort can do. It was wonderful," she said, "and we can do the same for Liz."

Joanne had joined in the cleanup, but she had her doubts.

Going to the slums was one thing. The ghetto women had probably watched, perplexed, as the suburban kids bustled in, scrubbed floors, sang songs, and then vanished, never to be seen again. Liz, on the other hand, would be back in touch with the crew as soon as the mess was once more out of control. Joanne made it her business to find Monica and recommend her highly. Liz could afford to pay for household help.

The manicurist arrived, a black-robed anorexic named Alexandra. After hugging everyone and passing out business cards, she got to work.

"What's a party without music?" Birgit asked. She turned on the radio, and she and Tamara danced. "That man who mugged you doesn't have power. *We* have power," said Birgit, dance rhythms urging on her speech. "Look at us, will you? Just *look* at us. People don't know how *together* we can be."

Women lounged on the bed while Alexandra worked on Liz. The acetone smell of nail polish mixed with the cigarette smoke, the flowers, and Tea Rose perfume until Joanne couldn't breathe. She went to the window, though she couldn't open it because of the air conditioning, and stood there, staring out through the lattice, at the street.

I I

Allison and Joanne had never spent any time alone together and didn't know each other well. Katharine sarcastically described Allison as a "crawler" — she couldn't meet you without getting all over you and covering every inch of psychic terrain. Joanne was a good listener, but she didn't like to talk about herself, and so Allison had not quite known how to get started with her.

But as they entered Sarah's building, they became allies. The hallway was cool by contrast to the street, and the sweat evaporated on their skins, leaving them tingling. In the moment before the still air reasserted its weight, they shivered together, sharing relief and a lifting of restraint.

"I've known Sarah for so long," Allison said. "I feel as though it's going to be *my* baby, too."

"If she doesn't marry him, she's going to need all of us," said Joanne.

"Even if she does marry him."

"Especially if she does."

Allison was much more excited; Joanne had Samantha.

Marty answered the door, looking almost childish, bare chested and in jeans. "She's not feeling well," he said. "She's resting."

"She'll see *us*," said Allison, the way she would with a secretary who didn't yet know which calls to put through.

Marty was too slight to block the doorway. Still, he hesitated, only a moment, before he stepped aside. He had lived with Sarah for three years, but she wasn't sure she liked him well enough to get married, and she *did* like the idea of no one but herself having any permanent say over her child. That was the way Joanne had done it and everyone said it had worked out fine. Samantha was wonderful.

Sarah was on her back on top of the sheets of the double bed. She wore a cotton gown and had a hand-held battery-operated fan pointed at her chin. She and Marty thought air conditioning was unhealthy. Perspiration ran down her face.

"We're here," Allison said.

Sarah moved in response, but without changing position. "I feel awful," she said.

"But you look wonderful," said Allison, stroking her friend's arm, since Sarah didn't sit up enough to accommodate a hug. "That eight-and-a-half-month belly of yours is the most beautiful thing I've ever seen."

In fact, Sarah was haggard, her eyes ringed with dark circles and red-rimmed from crying. She reached for the sheet and used it to wipe her neck.

"You should indulge your emotions," said Joanne, sitting on the bed. "Even the negative ones." The mattress shifted beneath her and for an instant the humid air shifted, too, a breeze. But then it vanished, the mattress pegged itself again to Sarah's back, and all she felt was the heat of another body nearby. She aimed the fan briefly at Joanne in a gesture of welcome. "Enjoy the self-pity," said Joanne. "Wallow awhile. It's your last chance. You won't have time for all that once the baby's born." Joanne liked to think about how much she had changed since Samantha's birth, how much she had grown. "What you need is a sponge bath," she said. "How does that sound? I'll wipe you down with something cool . . ." But she made no move to get up, and so Sarah didn't bother to tell her no.

"Liz wanted to come," began Allison. "But she was mugged last night."

Sarah expressed shock and Allison told the story. "Everyone was there today," she concluded. "It was wonderful, the way everyone rallied round."

Then they were silent, listening to sounds from the street, the whir of the fan, their own breathing. The rest of the apartment was strangely still.

"What do you think he's doing out there?" whispered Joanne.

Sarah sighed. "Probably reading *Natural Childbirth.* Again."

Allison took her new Minolta out of her tote bag.

"Well, I'm glad Liz wasn't hurt," said Sarah, "but to tell you the truth, I'm glad she didn't come."

"What do you mean?" asked Allison.

"She intimidates me. I've always been afraid of Liz."

"But why? Liz *likes* you."

"Liz is wonderful," added Joanne.

"I know Liz is wonderful. But I can't help feeling that she must despise me. Or if she doesn't, that she should. That she would, if she stopped to think about it."

"What do you *mean*?" asked Allison. "Liz isn't like that. Besides, you're wonderful."

"Liz would have kept working right up to delivery," said Sarah.

"Oh, please," Joanne objected. "Can you imagine Liz with a child, let alone pregnant?"

"But Liz would be a wonderful mother," Allison insisted.

"Liz is ancient," said Sarah, and Joanne and Allison knew what she meant. Liz was not a New Woman of the era, successful because success was in style. She seemed a throwback to some earlier time, when the only women to make it were those with real, palpable, exceptional power. "She's scary," added Sarah.

"Liz," said Allison, "is a very warm, caring person."

"Who must think I went and got pregnant because I'm not much good at anything else."

"That's not *true*," said the visitors.

Allison regarded Sarah's belly; Joanne, her face. If Sarah had any self-confidence at all, thought Joanne, she would have broken up with Marty long ago. It was important to make her understand she was as good as anyone else. So she said, "It's hard to imagine anyone mugging Liz. Having the *nerve*." Allison laughed, as if to acknowledge after all that she had been intimidated at times by Liz, too. Joanne felt guilty for making a joke about such a thing, but Sarah smiled and that made it all right.

"There, don't you feel more comfortable out of bed?"

Sarah stood in profile by the window. The security grate behind her cast diamonds of light on the floor.

"It's perfect," said Allison. "Oh, the shapes! I'll shoot some right into the glare," she said. "For the silhouette." She made Sarah turn slightly and lift her chin. "But you seem so knotted up," she said. "I want to capture your joy. Your joy! Oh, Sarah, remember, you're peaceful, you're confident. You're the earth before creation."

"I'm a sweating mess," said Sarah.

"God, it's all so wonderful," Allison whispered, soothing, circling around. She moved with her legs slightly bowed as though she'd had rickets as a child, which, considering her background, was unlikely. Joanne watched and thought the posture intentional. She found it a strange affectation though she could see it gave Allison a provocative edge. Allison could have been merely pretty. "Relax," said Allison. She crouched on the floor, focusing the lens. "Wonderful!" Click. "Turn a little. I want it from every angle. With the different shadows and all." Click. Click. "That's right, with your hands folded over. . . . Why don't you take off your nightgown?" she asked. "If I could get the *flesh*, it would almost be like actually taking a picture of the baby. You'll show it to her someday. Tell her Aunt Allison took it while she was still inside." She stood, blew the air out of her cheeks, and waited for Sarah to undress. "Are you getting anyone to film the birth?" she asked.

"I'm really not feeling well," said Sarah. "I think I'd better lie down."

"A couple more shots. You'll regret it later if we don't take them now. Joanne, help her get that thing off. What an incredible image — the belly and the breasts . . ."

Sarah sighed, or maybe belched, her disorder of spirit and body closely allied these days. She didn't resist when Joanne drew the light cotton gown up over her head. The hot air touched her skin, almost tickled, so that she felt a shiver that turned quickly to nausea, the fear of throwing up or of not being able to. Voices reassured her, Joanne reminding her she had only a couple of weeks to go, Allison saying just a couple more shots.

"My breasts . . . *hurt*," said Sarah. "All the time."

"What's the latest name?" Joanne asked, to distract her. In response to a gesture from Allison, she pulled the waistband of Sarah's panties lower on the hip. "That elastic's awfully tight," she said. "And in this weather. You'd be more comfortable without underwear."

"I've been thinking . . ." Sarah spoke slowly, one word at a time. ". . . Hephzibah."

"Hephzibah," the visitors repeated in unison, cautious and not entirely pleased, rolling the syllables on their tongues like a new vineyard's wine.

"If it's a girl," Sarah added.

"I *know* it will be a girl," said Allison. "But why don't you let the doctor tell you?"

"Hephzibah," repeated Joanne.

"I thought," said Sarah, "it would go well. With all the Zoës."

"Yes," said Joanne, enthusiastic now. "It fits in, but you won't have every kid in the sandbox running to you when you call *Hephzibah*."

"I think you should name her after Liz," said Allison. "Wouldn't it be wonderful? To have Liz as a sort of godmother?"

"Liz intimidates me," said Sarah, now decisive at last, returning to bed. "Can I have my nightgown?"

Allison snatched it from Joanne's hand. "Why don't you lie down and take off those stupid panties and I'll get a few more shots."

"How about Elspeth?" Joanne suggested. "Inspired by Elizabeth, but it takes the *Liz* right out of it. You know, to sort of defuse her."

"God, this is wonderful," said Allison, shooting from the foot of the bed. "It would be even better if you'd take your fig leaf off." She circled the bed, taking close-ups, moving in. Sarah had one hand on her stomach, as weak a defense as the arm she flung over her eyes: the classic female victim. Allison caught the pose. Click. She circled the bed, hungry. She imagined she could smell the baby, she could see it, it could not evade her. Sarah began to cry.

Joanne was holding her and rocking her clumsily when Marty came in.

"Are you all right?" he asked.

Allison motioned him aside and framed the scene, friend comforting friend.

"She's had a rough couple of days," Marty said. "You two better go and give her a chance to rest."

Allison sprawled back on the bed and faced him. She let the skirt of her sundress ride up, waiting to see if he would be a pig or a wimp. She smiled when Marty looked away.

"I think you'd better go," he repeated.

"I think that's for me to decide," said Sarah. She stopped crying long enough to lift her head from Joanne's shoulder and fix him with a look.

"What do you want me to do?" he asked.

"I want you to leave me with my guests."

Marty stood a moment, considering. "OK," he said at last, and left the room.

"Oh, I can't stand it. I just can't stand it," said Sarah, finding energy for the first time. "That's how he always is. He deals with any disagreement, any confrontation by simply running away. And later, once you leave, he'll sulk me. I know that's what he's going to do. I can't stand it anymore. I swear I would rather go through this alone."

"Well, you're not going to go through anything alone," Joanne said. "You have friends. You know that."

"Why doesn't he go?" asked Sarah. "There's a million single women out there. He could move in with any one of them. I wish he would. I really wish he'd just go."

"Let's vote on it," said Allison.

"On what?" asked Sarah.

"Her name," said Allison. "On the baby's name."

III

Allison and Joanne sat at the counter in the Copper Kettle.

"I feel great," said Allison eagerly. "I'm finally over him. I'm free." She hunched over her coffee cup, in a posture as far from liberation as Joanne could imagine. "Liz was wonderful through the whole thing, when I thought I would die — kill myself or die."

Joanne wished the conversation would wind up so she could get back to her daughter. Samantha had stayed behind and Joanne felt as though the girl was being held hostage: she wouldn't get her back until she returned and gave Liz more time.

"I'm a jealous person to begin with," Allison said. "A passionate nature. What can you do? But with William the Conqueror, I had *reason* to be insecure! Whenever he wasn't with me, I imagined him with other women. I used to imagine the look on his face when he was making love to them. Good ole Billy the Conk."

She's not over him, thought Joanne. If she were, by now she'd be calling him just Bill.

"Men!" Allison said. "Now I finally know the only hold they have on me is erotic. You can't let someone else become the center of your life. It doesn't work."

Joanne knew. She remembered how it used to be, to love someone to the point of obsession. All that anxiety! Whatever you did, someone else might still please him more. It was never enough.

"You were smart," said Allison, "to go ahead and have Samantha without being involved with a man."

More than ever, Joanne wanted to get up and leave. She thought of Allison circling Sarah on the bed, as though she would tear the baby out of the womb and chew it up right in front of them. The woman was so hungry. Joanne felt Allison would close in on her, maybe even on Samantha, if she didn't throw something her way.

"I felt cheated when Samantha was born," she said in a

confidential rush, half-convinced that Allison was about to put a hand on her knee. "She was born by cesarean. An unnecessary cesarean. They do that to women lawyers a lot, they're so afraid you'll sue if anything goes wrong. I was so angry, I decided to sue the obstetrician anyway, for cheating me out of my right as a mother. I wanted to be a *mother*. I wanted to give *birth*."

"How terrible," crooned Allison, happily. "You must have been so disappointed." She looked at Joanne's face attentively, then poured cream and sugar into her empty cup and sampled the mixture with her spoon.

"Talk about postpartum depression!" said Joanne. "But it was the last depression of my life. I had to pull myself together — for *her*." Joanne smiled; she had managed her life so very well. "And I'd better get back to her," she concluded.

She'd been gone almost three hours. What had Samantha been doing all that time? She'd been with Liz. Liz again. What was it about Liz? Samantha always loved to visit her aunt Liz.

It's the *cat*, Joanne decided in a panic. She likes the cat. I'll get her a kitten, she resolved, undoing the fingers that gripped at her heart. "Sorry to cut this short," she told Allison, "but the weekend is really all the time we have together." In the office, or even sitting in a deposition or a courtroom, her mind was always on Samantha, seeing her with teachers, the sitter, her friends, wondering, always, who was making her smile.

Little boys still run; little girls still skip. On the way home, Samantha's skirts billowed up and then brushed back

against her legs. Her ponytail flew out behind her and then
fell on her back, giddyap, giddyap. She went into a canter.

Joanne had thought of a more streamlined look for her.
Something straighter, more directed. Of course, she was
perfect as is, but it bothered Joanne that her daughter insisted on skirts.

"Samantha, come walk with your mother!" she called.
"This is *together* time."

The girl looked over her shoulder and smiled, but didn't
stop.

"Watch where you're going!" cried Joanne.

Samantha's skirts ballooned around her, buoyant and
promising. They might lift her right into the sky.

"My birthday's coming up," called Joanne. "That means
you're supposed to be nice to me."

Samantha skipped on ahead.

"Samantha!" The child looked as though she could fly.
"Come here, *now!* Your mother needs a hug."

Sophisticated Ladies

The night before I made the date with the twins, I was cooking dinner and decided to pour a splash of sherry into the sauce. It was good sherry. I'd bought the bottle because the man I really and truly loved drank nothing else. But the man was no longer in my life, and since I do not drink sherry myself, all I could use it for was cooking.

As I poured, the saucepan overflowed and the alcohol caught fire. I froze, too shocked to move, and so the liquid kept spilling into the pan and flaming up around my fingers as far as the wrist. My hand was wreathed in flames, but I wasn't hurt. The sherry evaporated instantly as it burned, and I watched in horror and delight while the fire blazed around me for timeless minutes, as hypnotizing and miraculous as the love had been.

When I finally managed to tilt the bottle back and stop the flow, and stood there in the kitchen examining my unburned hand, I should have felt lucky, but instead I felt cheated. All I could think of was how much my onetime friend would have loved the story. It was an anecdote that lent itself to the kind of metaphysical metaphor he enjoyed, and it had happened with *his* sherry, and it didn't seem right that I would never have the chance to tell him.

I walked across the room and pressed my face against the cold windowpane, my home remedy for the blues since I was a kid. Like many home remedies, it rarely works.

A car had broken down at the corner, its yellow emergency lights flashing in time with the Don't Walk sign, which was also on the fritz. The moon that rose over the bodega was yellow, too, a thin bright crescent that would have been more at home in a summer sky. Summer! I would be more at home in the summer, too. *Something* to look forward to! Once the warm weather comes . . . I told myself. Yeah, then what? Well, the windows would all open and everyone would be out on the stoops again with six-packs and radios. No more lonely nights. Anytime I wanted to, I could slow dance in the street — on roller blades, of course — with Ready Freddy. Was that enough to live for?

In the meantime, there was nothing left to do but play my tape of "Love Has No Pride." "What the hell's the matter with you?" I hollered at Linda Ronstadt. "You shouldn't get down on your knees for *any* man." But I had to agree with her: I'd do anything to see him again.

The twins are Annie's teenage nieces and Annie is my friend from the office. We work nine to five and as much overtime as we can stand. Nights and weekends are devoted to shopping for food and doing the laundry and checking in with our mothers on the phone. When Annie smiles, her beautiful black face lights up as bright as the city at night. It's such a dazzling effect, you can't imagine any man would ever want to see her cry. Which just goes to show how limited a woman's imagination can be.

The office we work in isn't bad, but it's not what either one of us had expected from life. Annie had been in school, but then the money ran out. I'm a writer, which means I've finally got up the nerve to call myself one though I'm not making a living at it. But because I've proclaimed myself a writer and because Annie gets dressed up every morning and takes the train from New Jersey into Manhattan, we were convinced that no matter how disappointed we might be with ourselves, we were still fairly glamorous in the eyes of the twins.

The twins are from the lost generation that isn't supposed to know how to read or write. They're supposed to be having babies instead, when they're not on the street watching drive-by shootings, that is, and keeping all the decent hard-working folks scared for their lives. They calmly ignore all these expectations, however, and go right ahead reading everything they can get their hands on. They also write smart, vivid stories and poems, from the heart. Annie had been passing their work on to me for a couple of years, and though the kids and I had a correspondence going, we had never met.

At any rate, the day after my near-disaster over the saucepan, Annie and I were talking during a coffee break when she said, "The twins want to meet you."

I panicked. To these two kids from Newark, I was a Writer. How could I meet them? I didn't want to rob them of their illusions.

The twins were so young and they seemed so fresh and eager. They didn't *know*, and I didn't want to be the one to tell them. Maybe they wouldn't ever have to find out. They might end up leading charmed lives and maybe everything would always work out for them the way they hoped. I remembered one of their stories, about first love in the school cafeteria. After I read it, I sat there very quiet and hoped that the girl who wrote it would never be hurt.

But at the same time, what did I know? The twins also wrote poems about divorce and heartache, about racism, about rape and crack and guns, about the fear of walking home after dark. So they were young. So what? Kids feel pain, too. And what do I know about what it's like to be growing up black in Newark? Where did I get off feeling so protective?

Years ago, my friend Renata took me to meet a glamorous old lady, a Hungarian émigré who had been a renowned beauty in her youth. Renata dressed carefully for the visit in a new lace-trimmed blouse with the top three or four buttons stylishly undone. We sat on a sunny balcony overlooking Central Park while the glamorous lady told us tales of love and illicit passion in a breathless, thickly accented voice. The diamonds on her hand flashed as she reached out and buttoned Renata's blouse chastely up to the throat.

Old ladies are entitled to such ambiguities. I wanted to claim that right. I'm not afraid of being old. I've always suspected I won't hit my stride till I'm fifty.

I wanted to amaze the twins and be big in their eyes. I could do it. They would love my New York apartment with its exposed brick walls — the sort of place a writer ought to live in. They would love to hear me tell of love affairs, all in a tone of dry humor and restraint. I was sure that the twins would consider me — at thirty — more than middle aged, and I hoped they would find it utterly bohemian that an old lady could still even think about love — and that she could talk about her disappointments without the tears and obvious torment of the similarly afflicted adolescent. I'd put on a good act, tell a good story, put some artistic distance between me and my suffering.

Unfortunately, I didn't really have many stories to tell about myself. Well, I could tell the twins about Margaret.

Margaret is an amazing lady of eighty who can outwalk, outtalk, and outthink *anyone*. Several months before I met her, Margaret had made a trip to Africa alone.

One day she bought herself a first-class ticket on an Algerian train. The first-class compartment was separated from the hot, overcrowded general car by a plate of clear glass, so that Margaret, seated in an otherwise empty car, could see the unwashed multitudes jammed together only a few feet away. She was embarrassed by such ostentatious luxury and such disparity in treatment, and was relieved when another first-class passenger came to claim the seat next to hers.

After a few pleasantries, the man inquired, in French, if Margaret knew what love was. From the safe vantage point of old age looking back on the passions of youth, she sighed, *"Mais oui,"* at which encouragement the gentleman attempted to mount her. She successfully fought him off with sharp kicks and fingernails while the teeming masses pressed up against the glass door, able to watch and shout, but not to help.

I hoped that at age eighty, I would still be ready to strike off across strange continents and take care of myself, and I wondered if I would also have the pride to resist what was most likely a last chance.

"Well, if the kids aren't doing anything Saturday night . . . ," I suggested to Annie.

Maybe we'd have a good time. They had an image of me, and it might be fun to try to live up to it. I could tell them the story about the sherry. *They*, at least, might enjoy it.

Saturday night, Annie and I walked into a club to hear a singer named Linda Alexander, who was billed as "Not So Nice." Annie and I didn't feel like being "nice" anymore either. The twins had stood us up.

Apparently we needed them a lot more than they needed us. Annie had phoned me with the bad news: the temperature was dropping, the forecast was snow, and the twins thought it was a perfect night to forget about weekend plans and just stay home.

I had already ironed my one decent shirt. I had gone over my budget six times till I'd pared off enough money for a night on the town. I was ready to get out, and instead I was going to spend the weekend doing laundry and sitting home. I sat there holding the phone.

"Why don't *we* do it?" asked Annie.

What? Spend money on ourselves instead of the kids? Play at being glamorous without the twins to applaud our act?

But really, why not? Let the kids stay home and watch TV, I agreed. The crazy old ladies were going to stay out all night.

"Not So Nice" Linda seemed perfectly nice to us and with an attitude I figured we could use a piece of.

I'm calling NEXT! on the happiness line.

she sang.

That's right, I thought. New York's a big place. Take a number and get on line. You better believe you could miss your turn if you don't holler "Next!"

"Annie," I mumbled, "the problem is, we've never learned to holler."

I was really enjoying the show. It seems I always turn to music to authenticate my life. There's a letter I treasured for years. At the bottom he'd scrawled a quote: "*I love you more than words can say.*" — — Otis Redding. That *dash dash Otis Redding* is what made me believe it.

Annie understood. She told me about a fight she'd had with a boyfriend. "I thought I was expressing myself clearly in my own words, telling him what I wanted from him. But then I got to the part where I went right ahead automatically and started spelling it out: *R-E-S-P-E-C-T*."

Linda Alexander looked right at us:

> *My friends have got what they want and I'm glad.*
> *Still I'm impatient for what I ain't had.*
> *I'm calling NEXT! on the happiness line.*

Later, we rolled around the Village and stuck out our tongues to catch the flurrying snow that had kept the twins at home.

"Calling next!" Annie cited our new authority, waving her hand and inadvertently hailing a cab.

At the next corner, people were dancing clear out to the street to live music, a hot blend of everything that everyone had grown up with — blues, country, and good ol' rock 'n' roll.

"Mmmmm," said Annie. "It's the blue note that makes it real music."

I was drunk enough to reply, "It's the blue note that makes it real life."

She was drunk enough to agree with me.

"But tonight," she added, "what they're doing, what they're proving, is you can have it blue and upbeat too."

We pushed our way into the club and up close to the Gillette Brothers Band.

Don't tell me the bad news,

sang Pipp Gillette.

Just tell me you love me . . .

"Mmmmmm," said Annie.

We ended the night in a jazz loft five long flights up, where the jam session started at 2:00 A.M. and breakfast was served at 4:00. We warmed our hands over hot cups of coffee and satisfied our hunger with bagels.

Annie and I felt on top of the world even as we stumbled down the stairs, two sleep-deprived secretaries with we hoped enough money to get home. But Annie did look glamorous in the light of the streetlamp, halos of snow around her head. I wished I had a camera so we could preserve some evidence, something to prove at least sometimes we can *be* our images. It's so easy to lose heart day-to-day, and then you need something — a photo, the music, or maybe someone else's expectations — to bring a good vision of yourself back.

"Thank the twins for me, OK?" I said. "I had a wonderful time."

The night had started with what I imagined to be their image of me; in the end I had claimed it, and as we headed uptown, I was jubilant. I stuck out my tongue to catch snowflakes, and so did Annie. For sophisticated ladies still open to simple pleasure, what more obvious image could you find?

But even as I merged with my enviable reflection, I felt a second-thought tug: it shouldn't be this way. Do I need somebody watching to make these gifts matter? Though I'm telling it now, I wish I didn't feel the need to tell it: the occasional wonder of the music, and Annie's friendship, the bracelet of fire that could not burn my hand.

Or do I simply want to share it? The last number in the jazz loft when a man in a bus driver's uniform got up and gave us "Ain't Nobody's Business," slow and off-meter, unfamiliar. The piano rushed it at first, the drums lagged a beat behind, the bass slipping out a sound, the horns nudging out notes, tentative, and nothing fitting. It made me ache — the bumpy real-life disconnection and the man's hoarse voice, the way he had to stand there, his hand marking out the tempo to a band that didn't get it. Then suddenly, the tenor sax was playing perfect counterpoint, the alto running up scales like a hand moving up my thigh, out of nowhere and improbably great. And later when the instruments dropped off, silent, the singer went on alone until the whole band joined him to end it, all of them tight for the moment and together. The ache stopped hurting. It rose through me, opening up in answer as they called it a night, calling up that constant possibility: impermanent joy.

Little Virgins

My landlord has been renovating the economy hotel he owns, a dark two-story building near where the marketplace used to be. Indians selling produce and handcrafts always liked to stay there, and commercial travelers on tight budgets did, too, until the government got worried about traffic congestion and moved the market to a covered hall away from downtown. There were few windows in the hotel and those were small and located high at the tops of the cells. Many looked out on other walls and air shafts. The interior was painted a dark sort of turquoise-green, like an aquarium or the bottom of a swimming pool seen through tinted glass. Cool and dark as a cave, admitting only minimal light, this was the sort of room Mexicans liked and North Americans wouldn't go near. So Don Carlos has been knocking out walls, opening up space for new windows to let in the relentless sun, letting the glare reflect off the whitewash and fresh paint.

We sat in the patio drinking Cokes in the midst of rubble while workmen pounded the walls. Carpenters cut lumber with handsaws and the sawdust filled the air with sweet pungency.

"You see," said Don Carlos. "I know what North Americans like."

"Everyone knows you do," I said politely. Everyone knew that my landlord had been a poor, illiterate, but good-looking young man in a godforsaken village when he managed to get an American anthropologist pregnant. *Poor thing,* everyone said. *Of course she was lonely, there all alone. These are the things that happen.* Of course, it was also a disgrace. The only way the American anthropologist was able to stay in the village long enough to finish her fieldwork was to marry her lover. She taught him to read and write and keep accounts, took him to the city and got him started in business before disappearing back to the United States with their child. People said no one had ever heard from her again, though others claimed she continued to advise Don Carlos on his finances — the only explanation for his success.

Don Carlos must have been fifty years old when I met him, but his hair was still black. While he knows all the social graces and these days moves among the finest people, he occasionally — as he did the day I went looking for him — likes to show his strength and recall his roots by removing bottle caps with his teeth. I like him. Aside from the initial American capital, he's a self-made man, also intelligent and charming. The anthropologist had not made a bad choice. Don Carlos is the only businessman I've ever respected. He isn't greedy for money; he loves his work. He loves to watch transformations: in his small factories, cloth turns into clothing, dough into tortillas, glass and plastic paste into rosary beads. And while his hotel may indeed make more money catering to Americans, I think Don Carlos began the renovations just because he craves change.

"Don Carlos," I said at last. "When I got home last night,

there was a strange woman in the house. She was cooking dinner on the stove and —"

"Yes, you mean Rosa," he said. "She's a simple girl from the village so I know you're going to like her. I felt so sorry for you living all alone."

"But you see, I want to live alone," I said, hoping he would simply respect my wish, though I know the desire is one that few Mexicans can understand. My Spanish is more or less fluent, but if there's a word for *privacy*, I cannot tell you.

"It is a big expensive house for one person," said Don Carlos. "It's better if Rosa helps you pay."

The "big" house in question is a single room with a high ceiling and exposed rafters — a converted storage shed stuck in a neighborhood of villas and mansions. A neighborhood designed for rich people, it's not my style. With no convenient public transportation, it's not what I would ordinarily choose. When I lived in Mexico before, I preferred the company of the poor. But life here can be hard on a single woman. You have to watch your step and so I'd seen the advantage to the exclusive enclave: my old friends would not be comfortable visiting me there. Not only would I be left alone for days at a time so I could concentrate and write, but my private life would not be open to their eyes. With luck — and without a roommate — I could get a lot of work done, keep my reputation, and still get away with the occasional love affair.

"I thought you would be friends," said Don Carlos. When I didn't answer, he sighed. "Ay, Rosa, what will become of you? . . . I will find her another place," he promised.

I stifled the American impulse to ask *When?*

That evening, Rosa had visitors, three men who came bearing suitcases tied up with rope; a bedstead for the mattress she'd previously put down on the floor; a couch upholstered in torn orange fabric with springs protruding and stuffing coming out. Two giggling young women stayed out of the way of the heavy moving, but they had their job, too — carrying bottles of Coca-Cola and brandy and rum.

The night before, Rosa had confessed — with a mixture of hesitant caution and bravado — that she'd come to the city following the man she loved. She'd stood there at the stove, potbelly bulging out of her shiny dress, not at all self-conscious about her excess pounds. Maybe even proud, I thought, like someone who'd gone hungry in the past.

The lovers embraced, bodies rubbing and grinding in the sort of display that has become common in the parks and streets though decent families still try to keep their daughters inside at night. (You can see them — young women in high barred windows, waiting for admirers, looking like caged animals or holy statues in the side altars at church.) The men fondled their dates. One of the women, a girl, really, accepted these caresses in the old-fashioned way, standing still and — as if entirely unaware of the man and what he was doing — staring straight ahead, passive and profoundly untouched.

During a break in the kissing, we introduced ourselves and shook hands all around. One of the men — Rogelio — unplugged my typewriter to use the socket for his cassette player, loaded with Michael Jackson.

I withdrew to my bed at the far end of the room, thinking I'd write letters or read, but gave up when someone turned off the lights. The invaders danced, tossed down drinks. It was like a high school party when someone's parents aren't home, right down to the make-out sessions on the torn-up couch.

"Don't you dance?" Rogelio pulled me to my feet and led me to the others with slightly too eager hands. I went along, telling myself to be a good sport. Rosa would move out soon. And after all, hadn't I chosen this out-of-the-way neighborhood for just this reason: so that I could, if I chose, entertain men and drink too much without shocking my conservative friends?

Regardless of the beat, Rogelio only knew how to slow dance, grinding up against his partner, and seemed reluctant to take such liberties immediately with me. I did not encourage him. We shuffled awkwardly, only our fingers brushing from time to time, while the two other couples clutched each other, clinging tight.

When the tape at last clicked off, Rogelio went to flip it over and Rosa's boyfriend handed me a plastic cup.

"We live together," said Rosa, "and so we must drink together."

"Toast to your country," urged her boyfriend. "But then we'll toast to Mexico!"

"I'll toast to Mexico with pleasure," I said.

These words seemed to end whatever restraint they might have felt. I was maneuvered towards the couch and everyone sat around, leaning towards me, avid and close. "Tell me when you are going to _____" and each named his or her hometown. "I'll have my family prepare a room for you. Whenever you want to go, however long you want to stay. Whatever you want you can have!" Someone passed around tortillas and canned sardines.

"Isn't it true," asked the girl, "that we Mexicans treat the gringos very well? So tell me, why is it that you treat us so badly when we go there?"

The third man, whose name I could not remember, refilled my glass. "If you don't drink up, it's *desprecio*," he warned.

Desprecio: scorn. I knew not to give any hint of superiority or contempt. The first time I ate dinner in a Mexican home, many years ago, I sat in a dark, low-ceilinged mud hut and was served a bottle of Coca-Cola, a large bowl of black beans, a supply of tortillas that replenished itself as I ate. "Won't anyone eat with me?" I asked, but no. The family stood around, solicitous, refilling my plate, watching. And anxious to show my appreciation, afraid to give offense, I ate everything before me, gorged myself, finding out only later that my hosts had been unwilling to serve themselves until the guest was done; I had eaten the entire family's meal.

Now six pairs of eyes were on me. I gulped the brandy, afraid they would read disdain in more measured sips.

"A Mexican will give you everything," said Rosa. "But if you hurt our pride — beware!"

"And the Rockefellers?" someone asked.

"What about the Rockefellers?"

"Ah ha!" several voices agreed.

More drinking. I longed to escape again to my corner, but two people had already done so, making love on my bed. I pretended to pass out on the couch — a pretense not far from the truth — and eventually fell asleep.

Suddenly I was shaking, remembering another night when I'd awakened to find my body vibrating, everything around me tapping and humming, shaken by an unseen hand. People were shouting *Está temblando!* which I took to mean "she's trembling." I thought my manifestation of kinetic energy had been powerful enough to awaken and awe everyone sleeping around me. (I'd read Carlos Castaneda, after all, and took it for granted that Mexico would give me metaphysical powers more precious than America's rational force.) Then I realized people were concerned with the earth, not with me. I woke up fully and understood what was happening at the same moment as the quake passed.

Now the beat-up orange couch was creaking, an unfriendly mass of lumps and springs. A presence — some living energy — balanced itself on the broken arm, some entity whose pressure and weight made the wobbly legs tap against the floor. Years ago, a child in the orphanage told me about her *virgencitas*, tiny little Virgin Marys two inches high, who often appeared at night at the foot of her bed. They said nothing. They were just there, she thought, to let her know she would be OK.

"Are you sleeping?" Rosa asked. She stopped agitating the furniture and insinuated herself beside me, smelling of liquor and perfume. "Look, the others are all dreaming. Now it's just the two of us awake," she said. "Two friends, speaking frankly. So tell me the truth about your country."

But I didn't want to be friends with her. And I didn't want to talk about the U.S. — either to defend or to criticize. She was drunk and aggrieved; I was intolerant, sure that nothing I could say to her would satisfy.

"I've studied English," she said. "My pronunciation isn't so good but I read it as easily as . . . as Japanese." Her voice darkened: "You probably don't believe me . . . I had a chance to travel," she said, "oh, a few years ago, first class, of course, but in Texas they treated us like dirt. And we give you everything, everything!" (while I was a gringa, unwilling to share the house, claiming exemption from the rules of hospitality). "In Hollywood," she said, "I met the movie stars. I went to all the parties. Oh, the swimming pools! Oh, the champagne! I know all the movie stars," she insisted. "All of them. We all speak Japanese. Like them, I live for the moment." She laughed, then gripped my arm. "You look down on us," she said. "I know you don't want me here. You think I'm lying. You think the party we had tonight was more boring than what you're used to. But tell me" — she had me propped up into a half-sitting position, my shoulders pinned back against the couch — "tell me what you want and I'll give it to you!"

"Tranquillity," I whispered. "Silence. Solitude."

During my first visit to this small Mexican city, in 1969, I spent two months on *el Callejón de La Soledad* — which I translated, wrongly, as Solitude Alley — attracted by the name and by the poverty. The small muddy quarter of ramshackle shanties was one of the few downtown neighborhoods still without electricity or running water. It seemed as far as I could get from suburban America, the world that had elected Nixon and dropped napalm on Vietnam, a society guilty of both racism and prosperity.

On the Alley, most of the women worked as laundresses. Every morning, they wandered the town seeking dirty sheets door to door while the children spent the day carrying buckets from a distant public fountain. The Alley ran behind the church of Our Lady of Solitude, which accounted for (and took away most of the promise of) the name. As for the poverty, it was every bit as grinding as I could have hoped, wearing away everything about my life that I took for granted, destroying certain parts of my ego — the outward trappings that Americans consider self-respect — without ever putting me in immediate danger.

Privacy didn't interest me back then. For pennies a night, I slept on a mat surrounded by ten or twenty other people. I changed lodgings almost daily — not to improve my conditions, but because the community was anxious to share the wealth. After a few weeks, my body seemed permanently covered with a layer of valley dust. My clothes were wrinkled and yellowed and probably reeked. (I never figured out how the women managed to get the paid laundry so clean.) For a change, I wasn't instantly recognizable as a foreigner, but even that was not to last: I was discovered by the Catholic Action ladies who trooped along the muddy crooked footpaths seeking to do good. They never once told me — as my friends and parents back home tried to do — that my wallow in poverty was self-indulgent. They simply put me to work: teaching people to read, distributing birth control information and the condoms which these sheltered ladies thought a wonderful new invention, having never heard the opinion of the Pope. They seduced me, gradually, back to the middle class, deloused me in time to have lemonade with the Archbishop in an old convent turned into a museum. Water played in a stone fountain and I stood there, tall, pale, and thin, surrounded by my new friends — corseted ladies who giggled like schoolgirls and dressed in black.

You are here to study? people asked me.

Not to study, I would answer, *but to learn* — a distinction I soon stopped making. Besides being pretentious, it proved too subtle to grasp.

I left Solitude Alley to live with my new adopted godmother, a woman whose house was full of abandoned children and Alley kids she'd decided to sponsor and put through school. I became, briefly, her gringa foster child. I had special privileges, though. Not Catholic, I was excused from daily mass; an American, I was allowed to talk to boys, free to leave the house at will, unchaperoned.

Afternoons I wandered while poor people collapsed and slept and my devout middle-class friends rocked in front of their TV's, watching soaps, screaming with delight each time a woman was unfaithful to her man. I loved the provincial city: a few impressive government edifices and the cathedral surrounded by modest shops; the low adobe buildings with continuous block-long pastel walls that made the streets as cheerful and monotonous as a nursery school's corridors. On every corner, men sold popcorn — "little doves" — and ices; women offered jicama slices sprinkled with chile and lime, and mangoes peeled and mounted on sticks. The smells were pineapples, roses, tortillas frying in oil, the sweat of men and burros, a whiff of garbage and spoiled fruit, charcoal fires from the outskirts of town. There were dozens of churches, many with esplanades and open plazas. I would walk across in the hot white glare. The Mexican sun would burn out the last traces of the USA, that moral swamp. I'd stand not so much transfixed — which would mean pinned down — but light, and full of light, reprieved.

When I went home in the end, I brought back with me the idea of virtue like an invisible infection, a resistant strain of Third World parasite.

In the morning, I woke on the couch. Rosa lay on her own bed, asleep in her boyfriend's arms. Rogelio and his girl were on my bed, and the other couple was gone.

I dressed and left, walked a mile to the bus stop. I had to see Don Carlos right away.

Overnight, political graffiti (all in the same hand) had appeared on walls from one end of town to the other — those great expanses of adobe are irresistible as chalkboards — and the streets were full of soldiers. Some stood guard, others painted over the revolutionary messages, others flirted with me as I got off the bus and headed for my landlord's hotel.

Don Carlos was eating breakfast. He stood, obviously distressed, and asked me to join him. I'm not an important person, just a hapless tenant, and it was hard to see how my presence, even my displeasure, could have him so upset.

"Señorita," he said, "I have heard certain gossip. . . . The situation has presented extraordinary difficulties. . . ."

I tried to speak, but he cut me off.

"Señorita, please. . . . Let me say from the outset that what has happened was not my intention in any way. Rosa is a girl from my own village and so I wanted to give her a helping hand. You can't imagine how hard it is for people these days, with the peso worth nothing and costs so high." He paused, to let me think about my U.S. dollars, I assumed. "Your Solitude Alley was luxury," he said. "Today, people are living in the garbage dump. Whole families, hundreds of them. . . ."

I had heard this before. "Where is this dump, Don Carlos? I've never seen it."

He stared at me solemnly. Some sights are not for North American eyes. "Believe me," he said, "when I gave the keys to Rosa, I didn't know about her local connections. But now I understand she's a wild one, she indulges herself with certain corrupt *judiciales*. . . . Do you see my problem?" asked Don Carlos.

"Our problem. Really my problem," I corrected him.

"The neighbors don't like it either, and yet they understand. Rosa has *friends*. I don't dare ask her to leave."

"But I can't live with her. So *I'll* move," I said, though it was not what I wanted to do at all.

"Señorita, it's not that simple. I feel so very bad about this. But you must not move."

"Why not?"

"Because you are a North American." Don Carlos never uses the word *gringo*. "There's been talk about you. You make friends with people, well, not the people that tourists meet. And so some say you are a radical agitator. Other people say CIA. If you leave the house because of the *judiciales*, who knows what might happen. Everyone will believe you have something to hide."

"But that's ridiculous. I'm not —"

"I believe you, señorita. I understand that you people have many reasons for leaving your country and coming here. But other people do not understand. Your situation is delicate."

"I don't believe this!"

"You must, señorita," he said. "You must stay in the house with Rosa, at least for a while. For your own safety, for your own good."

The street in front of the cathedral is closed to traffic; workmen are spreading wet cement, then pressing down molds to create false cobblestones, painstakingly, one small grid at a time. Eventually, the city will look like the colonial gem the tourists expect. I sat on a park bench, watching the progress of the work, feeling sorry for myself and ashamed: an imperialist in search of primitive idealism, neocolonialist of the soul. I expected *better* of Mexico.

"Should I avoid my friends?" I'd asked Don Carlos. "Will I bring suspicion on them, too?"

"No," he said. "You must act as if nothing has changed."
But nothing was the same. I shouldn't be here, I thought. It was impossible to be an unobtrusive foreigner; I would never blend in.

"A person cannot escape her culture," my godmother told me once. "You cannot. Neither can I." She told me Mexican women were the most self-abnegating in the world. "It's not good that way," she said, "but can I change my character just like that?" Of course not. Maybe the next generation would be different; as for her, she still had a choice: "to give myself and suffer, or give myself and be happy, giving something to the world."

We lived in a rambling house with patios and porches, gardens with parrots and flowers and herbs. In the courtyard, big girls washed the little girls' hair and rubbed their braids with wedges of green lemon and lime. The girls slept two and three to a bed in the rooms and back-patio shacks. A few little boys camped on the covered porches outside our doors. The children went to school in shifts and made ambitious plans: *to be a doctor, a lawyer, to build a decent house for my parents, pay for my sister's operation, help my baby brother go to school.* My godmother had one full-time plus some part-time jobs to support them all. I gave English lessons and baked fancy cakes. With the children's help, she catered parties, and embroidered tablecloths, taught knitting and crocheting on the side.

Over the years I visited for a week or ten days whenever I had both the airfare and the time. Each time, my godmother had a new address, and each time the house was smaller though just as full of hopeful girls. As it grew harder to make ends meet, her sacrifice was more apparent, but now she dismissed it: "I'm really very selfish. I just hate to be alone."

I thought of that "selfishness" later, in Reagan-Bush-era New York, when there was nothing coy or ironic about greed. I had a check in hand from a completed assignment — enough money to cover a month's rent and not much more. In poor and virtuous Mexico, I figured I could live on it, happy, for half a year.

That's how I returned and ended up renting from Don Carlos. This trip, I didn't want to live with my god-mother and be all *that* pure, but I could hardly wait to see her.

I found her staying at the home of a cousin, with the latest entourage of girls. I asked about everyone I once knew.

"What's become of Lilia?"

"She's gone," my godmother said.

"Where to?"

"I don't know. She left without saying good-bye."

Rufi? Gone. Lupe? Gone. Balbina?

"She's married and lives in San Ildefonso, a village not far from here. I haven't seen her, though, or heard from her in a long long time." (I went to see Balbina: three buses out into the countryside, leaving behind the city trees in favor of cactus — the tall green poles the people use for fences, the flat bearded jade paddles, *nopal*. The Balbina I remembered had looked like an American cheerleader, energetic, with a quick and beautiful smile. I found her barefoot in a hut with a baby wrapped up in a shawl. She's gone backwards, I thought. But — progress! — there was a cement floor, the baby was clean, there was a big TV. I congratulated her on her marriage and home. She shrugged. "I have nothing to complain about," she said.)

"And the ones with me now," said my godmother, "they

take money from me for schoolbooks, and then they spend it on marijuana and fancy underwear."

"Why do people learn only the worst things from us?" I asked and then regretted the condescension. As though Mexicans needed a gringo model and could not discover how to be selfish, shortsighted on their own.

"I'm so sorry," I told my godmother.

"For what? I wanted to give those children a chance in life. They took it."

(The cousin took me aside. "She has *nothing!*" she told me indignantly. "Not even a roof over her head. All these years helping, helping others. . . . Do they remember her? Are they grateful?" She shook her bobbed head. "She's a secular nun, but she should have been a real one."

"At least she would have a home in the Church," I agreed.

"No, that's not what I mean. As a nun, she would be inspiring. People would say, *How beautiful!* But giving up her life like this, people just think she is a fool. . . . And where is she going to go now?" she asked rhetorically. "She could stay here with me forever, but not the lot of them. When my husband comes home from California, they've got to go.")

Virtue and generosity might be elusive in the world, but they couldn't just vanish. My godmother needed assistance; someone had to appear and help her. In the park kiosk, a military band struck up a march and I rose, an idea coming to me along with the fanfare. Don Carlos, I thought, redeem yourself!

He spends his mornings visiting the factories. I waited at the hotel until he returned for lunch, then presented the problem: "My godmother and the girls need a place to stay."

He didn't hesitate. He admired her tremendously, he said, and yes, if she didn't mind the dust and noise — it really wasn't so bad, he lived in the midst of it himself — until the grand reopening, she and the Eleven Thousand Virgins were welcome to stay at the hotel, free of charge.

I ran through the streets, a crazy gringa, on fire to tell my godmother the good news.

"They're gone," her cousin told me. "My husband returned and said they had to go."

"But where are they?"

"They used to live with La Presidenta. I told them to go back. *Her* house is big enough."

"You mean she's still alive?"

A grand old lady of almost one hundred years, La Presidenta claimed she'd once been courted by a gentleman who would surely have become President of the Republic had his life not ended prematurely under circumstances too painful (perhaps too sordid) to recall. Even years ago, when I first met her, she was a shut-in, a skeletal creature draped in black lace, a life-size version of the dolls people buy in the marketplace for the Day of the Dead. Once a week, the Catholic Action ladies took a bunch of children from Solitude Alley to the public baths, to mass, and then to pay a call on La Presidenta. She would hug and kiss her visitors and they would sit quietly on straight-backed chairs while La Presidenta rambled on about old age, sickness, and loneliness, and sometimes about her glorious youth. How remarkable those children were, sitting polite and attentive, watching the old woman with their big eyes!

A teenager answered when I knocked at the gate. She squealed and threw her arms around me. "Who am I?" she demanded. "Do you remember?"

"Elpidia!"

I'd known her only briefly during a visit, but how could I forget? On one of the rare occasions when La Presidenta passed around candies, Elpidia had taken a bite of her chocolate cream and murmured, "It's the most delicious thing I've ever tasted!" Then she carried the rest of it home, melting in her hand, to give her sister. I could hardly imagine it: a child who would take only one bite of the most delicious thing in the world. My godmother was impressed, too, and decided to sponsor both girls.

"So you're all here!"

"No," said Elpidia. "Just me. When we stayed here before, it was very bad. She accused everyone of stealing. She called us nasty little Indians."

"Oh!" I remembered one evening when a child, meeting La Presidenta for the first time, ventured to ask, *Were you married to Benito Juárez?* Juárez was on everyone's mind as the country had just celebrated the centennial of his death, which put him well before even La Presidenta's time. *What a thought!* she'd cried. *No, never! As though I'd love a dirty Indian like that!*

"She even made up a song," said Elpidia, "all about little Indians, stealing and smelling bad. Once we knew the words, she didn't have to sing it. She'd just hum it all day."

The rays of the sun stabbed my tired head. Elpidia linked my arm in hers and led me to the horrible woman's house. "She's a sick delicate old lady," she said. "Poor thing. She gets no pleasure in life. She doesn't know what she's saying most of the time. I've lived here, taking care of her, almost two years."

I said, "You still have a tender heart."

"I had to do something, you know. I kept failing at school."

"And your sister," I asked. "How is she?"

Elpidia shrugged.

We sat on the old sofa in the salon and I remembered Elpidia, a tiny child, sitting in the corner on a straight-backed chair, her feet dangling. Her braids would have touched the ground if she'd let them fall. She wore them tied up, doubled over, they were so long.

Thump! thump! thump!

Elpidia jumped to her feet. "That's the song. Now she just beats out the rhythm with her cane when she wants me."

I was almost too exhausted to feel outrage. Alone, I yawned and leaned back against the cushions. A sharp corner jabbed my back: an open book. Not just any book. *Capital* by Carlos Marx. The reader — Elpidia? — was in the midst of the chapter called "The Working Day," and the margins were full of notes in a childish, primary-school hand: Mexican statistics about rural-urban migration, mortality rates, hiring and layoffs in the construction trades. In quotation marks, the words "Social Darwinism," underlined, and followed by a question mark. This from the girl — if it was indeed Elpidia — who could not get past fifth grade. I replaced the book and closed my eyes.

Elpidia returned chuckling. "Oh, when she goes to the toilet — pain!"

I wanted to ask her about Carlos Marx, but what if she'd heard those rumors about me — CIA? Instead I asked, "So where is our godmother now?"

"San Ildefonso."

"Oh, then she's gone to stay with Balbina?"

"Balbina, no. It's a bad home. Her husband drinks and beats her."

"Poor Balbina. I went to see her, and I didn't know, but something felt wrong."

"Something was always wrong with Balbina," said Elpidia, without sympathy. "Oh, she always had plenty of smiles for Catholic ladies and gringas, but we knew her better. We lived with her. We . . ."

I didn't want to hear more. I thought of the cheerful Balbina I remembered and the young mother she'd grown into, with a baby wrapped up in a shawl. I'd stood in her house and said how sad it was, the way everyone had scattered, that no one went back to visit our godmother. Balbina shrugged and said, *Everyone makes his own path*, and that was that. I'd had so many illusions.

"You know," I told Elpidia, "when I was younger, everyone in America was idealistic for a while, and then it ended. When I first came here and found so much love and generosity, I didn't realize you were just in a utopian phase." I paused, thinking to define *utopian*, but she seemed to know. "Everyone was cooperating, you were helping each other, working together, and I didn't think it would end. All those virtues. I thought they were Mexican. And eternal."

Elpidia wasn't moved. "It's a new era," she said briskly, but then softened. "Our godmother was magnificent," she said. "She was wonderful. In many ways, I owe her my life. But look how conservative she is. She won't criticize the government — ever — and she's so religious and strict. She was the greatest — for her time and place. Not now."

Into the dustbin of history, I thought, but said nothing.

"I'm better off here with the old bitch," said Elpidia. "She can't climb stairs, you know, so she's stuck up there. I use the house. I invite the *compañeros* that I study with."

"But how do you stand her?"

Elpidia laughed. "She's terrible, but she knows she can only push me so far. Any further and I'll kill her." Her pupils were dilated. My godmother had shocked me once by calling this look *their atavistic stare*. "So you see my tender heart! . . . . Well, when you go to San Ildefonso," she said, "ask for Doña Eugenia. That's who they went to." I waited a moment more, hoping she would say, "And give our godmother my love."

Doña Eugenia was squatting in front of her cooking shack when I found her, roasting coffee beans on a round metal plate over a brazier.

"Smells delicious!" I greeted her.

In return, she cursed, impatient because the shells were taking too long to burn away. "No, they're not here," she told me. It was too long a trip for them. How could the girls get to school? She directed me to an address back in town.

I went from a Doña Elda to a Doña Leocadia. My godmother was a saint — they crossed themselves, then blew into their fists — a true saint, they told me, but alas, they weren't able to help her. How could I blame them? I didn't even want to share my house with *one* roommate. And I thought of the foster kids who'd run away without a word, insistent — like me — on freedom. Solitude Alley has been bulldozed, but I went searching through the new shanty-towns outside the city limits, skittish each time I saw a man in uniform. I looked for them at a construction site in a new

colonia where the sun went down and a soldier whispered
Let me go with you! and in a storeroom behind a corner store
with almost empty shelves. Anacleto works there now, a boy
who once slept outside my door and now considers himself
lucky with a few cents pay and space to unroll his sleeping
mat. He sent me to Don Raúl and his model poultry farm,
but it was a dead end. They hadn't been there.

We'd gone to a model farm years ago, the little girls all in
pinafores and plastic sandals. We saw two turkeys fighting — strange how those placid birds turn so passionate on
the attack — and one girl rushed into the fight and hobbled
the aggressor by grabbing and crossing its wings. The children scrambled into the guava trees in the orchard, gathering ripe fruit in their aprons, except for Elpidia, who
reached a crotch in the tree and seemed to forget what she
was doing there, smiling to herself and looking out at the
distant blue mountains and the sky. At the house where we
all lived, my godmother stood behind the wash trough on
Sunday, shampooing little heads: *Do we have lice? No, we don't
have lice. And why don't we have lice? Because we keep clean and
wash our clothes and our hair. And when you grow up, you'll keep
clean and you'll keep your husband and your children clean. And
how many children are you going to have? One or two children.
And when you're older, you'll learn how . . .*

How could they just vanish?

"It happens," said Don Carlos. He poured me another
copita. We were drinking by candlelight at his kitchen table: a
couple of glasses, a bottle, plastic flowers in a vase. (The
rosebushes in the courtyard had been trampled, were coated
with plaster and dust, and I wondered if they would survive.) "You should go home," he said.

I made a face at him over my glass. "I'm in no hurry to see our friends the *judiciales*."

"No. I mean to the United States. Go home, relax, make money."

Once my godmother had told me to go, too. "Help the poor people in your country," she said. I didn't do that either.

"There's a good life in the North," Don Carlos said. "Everyone knows."

"Depends what you mean by good.... Let me tell you about the kind of people I work for," I said. "There was this editor who stopped running my work because she didn't like my casual way of dress. But then her boss came upon something I'd written and had her secretary call me. She *loved* it, she was dying to meet me. So I borrowed a suit and a briefcase from a neighbor and went to meet the editor in chief. She doesn't even try to hide her disappointment. *Oh, she says, I thought you'd be wearing blue jeans and a black beret.*" I could see he didn't understand. "The last work I did was an article about a terrible childhood disease, a neurological condition that twists little kids up" — into pretzels, I wanted to say — "into ... braids.... And I found a doctor, Don Carlos, a world expert on this condition who's been treating children and curing a lot of them, too. He works in a hospital in Kansas City, Missouri, and I flew out there to interview him, talk to the kids, see him at work."

"Sentimental junk," said Don Carlos, surprising me. It wasn't for him to say, and besides, it had been a comparatively meaningful assignment as these things go.

"Two months later, the editor phones with a problem. She's confused. Kansas City is in Kansas. Why had I written *Missouri*?"

"There's a Kansas City on each side of the state line," said Don Carlos, expert on North American life.

"Yes, but the editor acted like she'd never heard of such a thing. *I'm a very educated woman,* she told me, *and if I find this confusing, our readers won't be able to deal with it at all.* They decided not to run the story, because the doctor lived in Kansas City."

"I don't believe it," said Don Carlos.

"Believe it," I said. "My big mistake was saying *So if people don't know about Kansas City, Missouri, run the story. They'll learn something.* There was a long silence on the other end of the phone. Then my editor — from that moment on, though, she wasn't my editor anymore — said, *I don't think you understand the function of this magazine.*"

"I didn't know," said Don Carlos. "I didn't know North Americans were so ignorant." He played a moment with his glass, his eyes closed, and I felt sorry for him, afraid his new perspective on America had somehow changed the way he remembered the woman who had loved and left him. He said, "You people are supposed to be so smart."

"People *want* to learn," I said. "I still believe that. We want to be better than we are. It goes so deep, it's instinct. I know a girl, a teenager," I said. "She keeps failing sixth grade. She's supposed to be slow. But she reads Karl Marx — "

"Yes, the Marxists take advantage of the economic situation," he said. "Distributing books, running study circles. . . ."

"You know what I think?" I asked him. "People embrace Communism because Marxists treat them as though they have brains. Marxists give them the chance to use this part of themselves they didn't even know they had. It's an awakening, and so it all seems like pure truth — the intellectual sensation is that strong."

"Ahhh, you are comparing it to sex," said Don Carlos, the first time that subject had come up between us. "Just as a woman loves the man who reveals her own body to her . . ."

"Yes," I said. "If she doesn't know the feeling is *hers*. If she thinks she can only feel it because of him. . . . Learning is an instinct," I insisted. "Don't people go wrong when their natural instincts are thwarted?"

Don Carlos poured another drink and laughed. "Sex produces a child and learning produces wisdom, but the doing of it is where the pleasure lies."

There was an awkward silence: Don Carlos, perhaps, thinking of his lost gringa and the child she had taken away; me wondering if he would turn out to be it — the discreet adult relationship I'd had in my plans.

"Well, I better go back to Rosa's," I said.

He grunted, unhappy that I was leaving or else displeased to hear me refer to the house as hers. Then, "It's late. I'll drive you."

The city is mysterious at night, dark, with no one out. The motion of the car soon made me realize how much I'd had to drink. I was too tired for this; what was I doing here? We took the peripheral highway and then the back way into the rich neighborhood I'd thought to make my home. The party was still going on, only now the music had changed — the cheerful wail of a *ranchera*.

We parked in front of the gate and Don Carlos put his

arms around me in something more intimate than the usual friendly *abrazo*. "Are you all right?" he asked.

"Just drunk," I said. "And sad."

"Maybe you shouldn't go in there like this."

"I'll be fine. Like this, I might even fit in."

He seemed reluctant to let me go. "Now, not a word about Carlos Marx to *them*. . . ."

"No, of course not," I said. "I'll just dance the night away in self-defense."

"We should go back. You could stay at the hotel."

"No," I said, but relaxed in his arms.

"Well, I'll walk in with you."

"No, no, you can leave me now. Go on home. I'll be fine."

When I first arrived in Mexico many years ago, I stayed briefly in a hostel in another town, and I stayed there longer than I intended because of a stone wall covered with vines and white flowers. *Nardos*, someone told me. The fragrance, if it hadn't been so perfectly balanced, would have been overpoweringly sweet. But it was perfect. A friend of mine says we get our idea of perfection from God, which I do not believe, but the perfume from those flowers did seem to impart some kind of grace.

Nardos. My dictionary said "tuberose," but when I returned to the United States, that turned out to be a funeral parlor flower with a rather musky, waxy smell.

Behind the house I rent from Don Carlos there's a ravine and in the thickety scrub, a broken stone wall over which *nardos* (if that's their right name) fall in profusion. The flowers are especially fragrant at night. They drew me — after Don Carlos drove away — to the ravine.

The full moon made everything glow as I plunged my arms among the vines. I touched a blossom and something moved in my hand, backing out of the flower like a bumblebee. For an instant, a little *virgencita*, no more than two inches high, hovered before my face, a golden aura lighting her robes. When I blinked, she was gone, but I knew — or imagined — the night was full of them. They weren't all Marys, either, not at all. Some wore pinafores and braids, shawls, corsets, even glasses, blue jeans and a black beret. The night was full of them, and the scent of white flowers.

"Where's my godmother?" I asked.

The air around me trembled and hummed: the *virgencitas*, little good-for-nothings, were silent, but Rosa's voice ascended, singing along with the music: mournful, then lusty; hot and high as flames from a house on fire reaching up up up just before the roof comes down.